DOS INDIOS

Harold Jaffe

DOS
INDIOS

THUNDER'S MOUTH PRESS • NEW YORK • CHICAGO

Copyright © 1983 Thunder's Mouth Press
All rights reserved under International and Pan
American Copyright Conventions
Published in the United States by Thunder's
Mouth Press, Box 780, New York NY 10025 and
Box 11223, Chicago IL 60611
Design by Ute Jansen
Cover photo courtesy of Magnum
Funded in part by a grant from the Illinois Arts Council.
Library of Congress Cataloging in Publication Data:
Jaffe, Harold
   Dos indios.
   1. Indians of South America—Fiction. I. Title.
PS3560.A312D6 1979   813'.54   82-25603
ISBN 0-938410-11-3
ISBN 0-938410-10-5 (pbk.)

Distributed by
Persea Books
225 Lafayette St.
New York NY 10012

for Maggie
who heard
and for Howard Sann,
friend and editor

DOS INDIOS

Everything the Power of the World does is done in a circle. The sky is round, and I have heard that the earth is round like a ball, and so are all the stars. The wind, in its greatest power, whirls. Birds make their nests in circles, for theirs is the same religion as ours. The sun comes forth and goes down again in a circle. The moon does the same, and both are round. Even the seasons form a great circle in their changing, and always come back to where they were. The life of a man is a circle from childhood to childhood, and so it is in everything where power moves.

BLACK ELK, OGLALA SIOUX

I THE QUENA

When the mist lifted, Manco saw that the small plaza was filled with people. He was on his father's shoulders listening to a man address the crowd. The man, whose costume was the color of clouds heavy with rain, held his odd-shaped cap in his hands and looked earnestly at the people. Manco heard the words "Dios" and "Cristo," which were familiar to him, though they did not sound the same coming from this man who blinked his eyes when he spoke. Looking about him, Manco saw that not only his father and mother and two sisters, but his relatives and all of his neighbors were pressed together, listening. Manco glanced from one face to another . . . The faces looked the way they did when they ate, very serious, without joy. Manco looked again at the speaker: he had done something to himself, his hair was too short on his head so that his ears stuck out. Nor did his body seem comfortable in its tight costume with the shining buttons and the enclosed shoes. Manco remembered another man he saw once with faded skin and hair the color of winter grass. The speaker reminded the boy of the faded man, though the speaker's skin was not faded, but was the color of earth, like Manco's own skin. It was something else, something in the speaker's manner.

Now he held his cap in one hand, and in the other held a cloth that fitted over his fingers:
"Brothers, sisters, this little doll I have in my hands can talk and sing. It can weep. Its name is Jesús Cristo." The speaker turned to the doll: "Weep for our brothers and sisters, Señor." He looked up again at his audience. "Jesús tells me that he cannot weep for you here because here is not the proper place. But if you promise to come to the Iglesia this afternoon at three o'clock Jesús will weep for you, and he will sing to you of his sufferings . . ."

Manco wondered why the speaker was addressing the people in Spanish and not in Quechua.

" . . . Jesús es el Generalísimo—Jesús is the great leader of the Salvation Army, my brothers and sisters. And everyone of you can become soldiers in this wonderful army if you promise forever to obey your general, who will address you this afternoon at three o'clock in the Iglesia."

At three o'clock Manco found himself sitting between his younger sister and his father on the high hard wooden pew-chair of the Iglesia. All of the people who had been in the plaza now seemed to be gathered here in the Iglesia to listen to the tiny doll called Jesús weep.

Manco was unhappy to be sitting on the hard Iglesia chair waiting to listen to this strange man speak to his fingers. It puzzled him that while he, a boy of six years, could see clearly how wrong it was to be there, the others, especially the adultos, could not see—

Manco's thoughts were interrupted by his ears which were hearing a music, a slow sad tune played on a wooden pipe. The music seemed to be coming from a place near to him, on his left, by the smaller eastern entrance to the Iglesia. Instead of turning to the sound, Manco closed his eyes to listen better. For several minutes he listened with his eyes closed. He had, he thought, heard this music before someplace, but here it sounded so fine: he felt as though his entire body were wedded to the proud, thin, mournful notes . . .

The next morning, soon after sunrise, Manco was out of his casita and running towards the mercado and Calle Chinchero where the quena-, or wooden pipe-makers, sat. The boy remembered having seen several of these old men squatting against the broken wooden structures, carving their pipes, painting them, bargaining with passers-by. But now, because it was so early, the quena-makers' corner was deserted. Not one of the men was there. Manco turned his body, scratched his head, then began, sadly, to make his way back to the casita. All yesterday, since hearing the tune on the quena in the Iglesia, he had planned his strategy, how he would approach the oldest, the most infirm of the quena-makers, and strike a bargain with him: he, Manco, would run errands, do tasks, even apprentice himself to the old man, in exchange for a quena. That was all that mattered, he must have a quena, he must learn to make visible the tune he heard in the Iglesia, which was whistling through his chest as if it were a songbird locked in a cage. To unlock this cage, to allow this small bird to regain its freedom, would not only give joy to Manco, but to his parents, to his relatives and neighbors, to all the people who were pressed together in the plaza and sitting stiffly in the Iglesia, without joy, listening to the man with the enclosed shoes speak to his fingers.

Manco was thinking that he would have to return to the mercado in a few hours to find his quena-man, when someone motioned to him through the mist from the other side of the gutter. It was one of the old women who sold herbs. When Manco approached her she looked him over, then said:

"It is early to be walking through the mercado, niño. Who are you looking for?"

"I am looking for the quena-makers," Manco answered. "I would like very much to have a quena so that I might learn to play it."

"I see. A quena sells for ten soles. Do you have ten soles, niño?"

"No, Señora."

"Do you have any money at all?"

"No, Señora."

"How do you expect to buy a quena without soles, child?"

Manco gazed at the old woman without responding. Then he said, "I can do tasks."

Manco thought she might scoff at this reply. She didn't scoff. She continued to stare at him.

Though he meant to say nothing, Manco said again, "I can do tasks."

"Come here then."

The old woman pulled the boy to her and beyond her through a narrow stone entrance.

"Go until you come to an opening."

The old woman nudged Manco into the corridor. It was very dark and damp and so narrow that Manco could feel the stone walls on either side of him. He did as she told him, moving without fear into the darkness. He continued for a longer time than he expected without coming to an opening, but then he saw something, light, ahead of him. The opening was in the wall to his left, quite low to the ground. Manco had to bend his body to enter.

He was in a small cell-like room which was surprisingly high, with a very small circular opening on one side where the wall met the ceiling. Wreaths of smoke gathered against the ceiling. Manco smelled the copal incense. The light that passed through the opening partially illuminated the room. An old man was squatting against the wall beneath the opening. He did not look up when Manco entered. For a few moments Manco stared silently at the old man. Next to him on a metal pan copal was burning. Manco watched the smoke rise and curl. Then he looked again at the old man. Finally he said:

"With permission, Señor, I am looking for a quena."

The aged man, his head on his chest, did not respond.

"The Señora herb-seller told me to come here."

No response.

"I am looking for a quena," Manco repeated timidly.

At this the old man raised his head and Manco saw that where his eyes should be were only pits. The old man's blindness frightened him.

But then the old man was grinning. Manco could see

his gums and threads of saliva suspended from his lip. He was gesturing to Manco to sit next to him against the wall.

The child sat.

The old man held a slim wooden pipe to his mouth. From the first note Manco was certain that he would hear the tune he had heard in the Iglesia . . .

When Manco emerged from the darkened corridor, the garúa-mist had passed. The day was bright and fine and the sun was high in the sky between the sierras. Manco placed the quena to his mouth and blew softly. The sound that resulted was broken, without smoothness. He tried again, covering the holes with his fingers. This time the sound was deeper, but still broken. Manco felt something in his mouth. He removed a few shreds of chewed-up coca leaf from his tongue. He smiled, thinking of the blind old man. He placed the quena to his mouth again, carefully covering the holes with his fingers, blowing softly. The sound this time was better.

Behind him he heard another sound, human, high-pitched. Turning, Manco saw a young man, his poncho wet and grimy, lying in a ditch in the gutter. His body was jerking and he was making whelping noises like an injured dog. Manco wanted to help him, but he did not know how. A voice from across the gutter said: "What is the matter, chico, have you never seen a drunken Indio?"

The man who said this was grinning. Manco felt the sun on his head and suddenly remembered that his parents would be concerned about his absence. It must have been several hours since he left the casita for the mercado. He secured his quena in his poncho and ran in the direction of his house.

That night, lying on the floor beneath the large poncho, between his two sisters who were already asleep, Manco reviewed the extraordinary chain of events which began with the appearance of the strange man from the "Salvation Army" in the plaza. The weeping fingers . . . the tune in the Iglesia . . . the deserted corner of the mercado in the garúa-mist . . . the old woman of the herbs . . . the long,

dark, damp corridor . . . the faint light . . . the aged man
with the pitted eyes . . . the very same music of the Iglesia
remarkably reproduced . . . the sun high in the sky . . . his
own futile attempts on the quena . . . the whelping noises of
the man in the ditch . . . the return to his casita, his father's
initial anger but eventual puzzled acceptance when Manco
explained what had transpired.

Now Manco had his quena, though the best he could
do with it so far was produce two sequential unbroken
notes. Just as Manco was about to fade easily into sleep,
two feelings took hold of him almost simultaneously. One
was connected with his remark to the old herb-woman that
he would be willing to "do tasks" in order to obtain his
quena. And the other had to do with the burden of the
small bird locked within his chest, whose release was somehow tied to the whelping, sorrowful cries of the "drunken
Indio." Neither these feelings nor what they meant was at
all clear to the boy, which might be why they produced in
him a vague, chilling sensation he had never before experienced, even as he exulted in his good fortune.

Manco's father was a woodcutter. Each morning at
dawn he would take his axe, his machete, his rope and his
sling and go off to the cone forest in the direction of the sun
above the city of Cuzco. One or the other of Manco's sisters
would always accompany him to help gather the wood.
The sister who stayed behind worked with the mother in
the casita, cleaning and weaving. On the first and last day
of each week both sisters and Manco would accompany
their father, because those were the days when the wood
was delivered to the shopkeepers in the hills of Cuzco. On
these occasions the father took a large amount of rope and
each child carried a sling to cart the wood. Manco looked
forward to these days in the forest, gathering the good-
smelling wood, glimpsing the brightly colored birds and
the small animals, hearing the crack of his father's machete,
feeling the strain of wood on his shoulders and the satis-
fying tightness of the sling about his forehead. Manco also
enjoyed observing the occasional joke and brusque remark
that passed between the shopkeepers and his father, seeing

the varied wares and the customers. It was on such a day a
year past that Manco had seen in one of those shops the
faded man with the hair the color of winter grass who
resembled the Indio who spoke to his fingers.

On the fourth night after Manco acquired his quena,
the boy was preparing to go with his father and sisters into
the forest to cart the wood. His sling and his quena, which
he was never without, were on the floor where he slept.
Manco imagined himself in the dawn walking behind his
father and in front of his sisters in the direction of the cone
forest, all the while playing on his quena the three smooth
notes he so far commanded. It was with such a thought that
Manco faded into sleep.

He awoke suddenly and long before dawn to the des-
perate screeching of birds. And then the room trembled
. . . and stopped. It trembled again, louder, deeper. Manco
felt his sisters and the earth that was his bed dance away
from him . . .

When he awoke the earth beneath him was strange
and the sun was slanting down on him without heat.
Manco looked up out of his eyes at a mud-caked roof he
didn't know. The eyes that gazed silently down into his
own belonged to an old woman, they were filmy, filled
with grief. The boy closed his eyes, knowing that all he had
ever lived by was lost. Utterly.

II COJO

$\mathbf{M}$anco's legs were gone. His
father, his mother, his two sisters were gone, buried somewhere in the broken earth. Manco's legs were gone. Thick
rubber pads were fastened to the stumps of his thighs, and
he moved painstakingly with the aid of forked sticks.
Manco now lived with his father's sister, Soledad, and her
family on the Altiplano, high in the sierras south of the city
of Cuzco. Manco's uncle was called Kero, and there were
four children, three boys and a girl. The father and all the
children were zagalejos, shepherds of their small flock of
llamas and alpacas. They also owned two pigs and several
chickens which stayed in and around their casita. The casita
was not made of wood like Manco's real casita in the city of
Cuzco, but of stone and clay and puna grass. It stood on the
treeless rock and wintry grass of the Altiplano, which was
closer to the sun than Manco's real casita, but did not seem
so because the air was thin and the wind bit into his face
and the clouds got into the way of everything and masked
the sun.

On occasion Manco went with the zagalejos, riding on
one of the llamas into the campo. Usually he stayed behind
in the casita with his aunt. Manco did not prefer one or the
other. In the campo he was useless and cold. In the casita he

was merely useless. His relatives, with the exception of Pepito, the youngest son, tended to ignore him. He was of no worth as a worker, another mouth to feed. Yet they felt a little sorry for him and obligated to his dead family. The best course in this awkward situation was to largely ignore his presence.

The children, especially the two oldest, were sometimes tempted to mock their cousin, and occasionally they gave into the temptation, jeeringly referring to him as "Cojo" or "Cojito," which meant cripple. Manco ignored them, as he ignored nearly everything connected to his new home. When Manco had lived in his real home in the city of Cuzco, he observed all things, took part in all things, and did not know fear. It was not that he felt fear now in this new place. Mostly he felt cold, a cold pressing numbness in his chest. The image that came to mind when Manco thought of this feeling was the ice that silently capped the peaks of the sierras encircling the Altiplano.

Pepito, the youngest boy, recognized something of himself in Manco. At seven years old, Pepito was a year younger than his cousin. And yet he was much younger, age having little to do with it. The kinship Pepito felt with Manco was not expressed in words, or even in gestures. It was expressed in the ease and rightness of their times together: sharing the docile llama's back on the ride into the campo; lying haunch to haunch beneath the heavy poncho on the earthen floor; eating onions and grain and potatoes from the brown cloth spread on the floor . . .

For Manco the seasons moved from clouds and cold and rain; to clouds and cold without rain; to clouds and rain without cold. In this last "season" flowers sprouted in the campo and outside the casita. Once, just after dawn, as Manco hobbled on his sticks out behind the casita to urinate, he was startled by hundreds of small blue flowers growing close to the grass everywhere about him. At once his mind lurched to the city of Cuzco, to an early morning there in the mist of the garúa, and to an old woman squatting, selling herbs . . . It took an effort for Manco to pull himself back to the Altiplano, to ice.

In the course of nearly three years spent in his new

home beneath the vast, gloomy sky, Manco's uncle Kero lost one alpaca and acquired two more llamas. Aunt Soledad fell ill and remained so for two months, in which time Manco's female cousin tended to her mother and to the casita. But then Aunt Soledad recovered, his cousin again rode off to the campo in the mornings, and all things continued as usual. Manco, for his part, did little of anything, scarcely spoke, and learned to keep himself from thinking without straining to do so.

One early morning in his fourth year, during the season of clouds and cold without rain, Manco rode into the campo with his uncle and cousins. Once in the shepherding area, he separated himself by hobbling off towards a large outcrop of rock in the direction of the sun. Though wearing a heavy alpaca poncho, Manco could not keep the cold from seeping beneath his skin. Moving, even slowly, was better than not moving at all. Time moved faster when he moved. Besides, though Manco had come to this same stretch of grazing campo many times in the last three years, he had never gotten to the outcrop of rock that formed a portion of the easternmost sierra. Until now he had never even thought of going there. Generally he occupied himself by hobbling fifty meters one way, then fifty meters back, until he grew tired. Then he sat on the hard ground and looked at the grass or the clouds or the grazing animals. And at midday he took lunch with his cousins, sitting next to Pepito, warming himself a little at the fire.

But now he found himself pushing east towards that portion of the sierra three or four kilometers away. Less than half the way, Manco realized why he had never before considered going there: it was a considerable effort. It would have been an impossible effort even six months ago. Manco had become stronger, more adept with the forked sticks he used as crutches. And still he was wet with sweat, wearier than he remembered ever being—though more than half the distance remained. He struggled for another fifty meters, then dropped his crutches and tumbled onto the ground. He lay on his back breathing heavily, feeling the wetness under his arms and on his face. He looked at the sky and the low dark clouds that had many forms. He thought:

"I, Cojo, am looking at the sky. Cojo is small and broken and colored the color of earth beneath grass. The sky is grey and endless and filled with clouds. What has the sky to do with Cojo? What has the sky to do with the others, the whole ones, my cousins and many thousands like them, who labor beneath it?"

This was the most elaborate thought Manco had framed in three years. It had come upon him unbidden. It disgusted him. He closed his eyes hard, feeling the sweat of his exertion beneath his eyelids.

"What has this cripple's exertion to do with the vast sky beneath which he exerts?"

He was doing it again. His head was doing it. Manco pressed his fists hard against his temples, and with his eyes closed lay that way without thinking. He lay that way for several minutes or longer, because the next sensation he felt was of heat pressing him against the earth. It was the sun. Manco gathered up his crutches and continued hobbling towards the mountain.

His short sleep must have refreshed him because he was moving faster, more energetically. Not only was he no longer tired, his body actually felt relaxed. Yet alert, confident. So confident that Manco almost felt that he could drop his sticks and walk without them, in the old way, as he did when he was a child in the city of Cuzco.

At one point, 200 meters or so away from the dark grey outcrop of rock, Manco heard a soft sound, as of wind murmuring through a forest of cone trees. This was not possible. The wind was still and the Altiplano nearly barren of trees.

Finally Manco was nearly upon what he had hobbled a great distance to get to: the large grey-black outcrop of rock that was a portion of the eastern sierra. About it was nothing, merely the hard dry puna grass and stone of the Altiplano. Manco was moving slowly now, his body was very tired. It had become colder. He was dreading the journey back to the pasture area. He paused: he was hearing music, the gently elongated strains of a harp. Manco did not understand. Yet the music was not altogether unfamiliar to him. And then he saw someone beneath the rock. A man playing a harp. Quietly, Manco made his way towards him. Sitting on a stone the man was bent over his small harp as if performing for an audience of princes, though about him as far as the eye could see was only the arid waste of the Altiplano.

When he was ten or fifteen meters away from the musician, Manco stopped. He knew the music. This awareness at once produced another, painful, awareness: he did not want to hear it, did not want to experience what this music contained for him. He did not know what the music contained, except that it was connected to his previous life in the city of Cuzco, to the cone forest above the city, to the garúa-mist . . . Manco wanted to leave. But he was exhausted, too tired to start back right away. Nor was there any point to it. The music, now that he heard it, would pursue him the entire way back. Instead he moved forward, closer to this bent musician performing to grass and cloud and stone.

Manco did not stop until he was but a body's length away from him. The man continued to play without looking up. Manco waited, trying to keep his ears, and his mind's ears, from focusing on the music. Manco was waiting for the tune to end or for the musician to acknowledge his presence. Neither happened.

Tired as he was, Manco had already turned around with the intention of starting back for the pasture, when the musician addressed him.

"Cojito," he said softly, without ceasing to stroke his harp.

Manco turned to him.

"Cojito," he said again without raising his head. The name that Manco hated but had learned to ignore, sounded in the harpist's lips as if it were a part of the music, so softly, so without mockery, was it uttered.

"Cojito, this what you are hearing is 'yaravi.' It is of the mountains. The mountain is born of the earth and brushes the sky."

Manco listened to the words, listened as much to their

sound as to their meaning. He found it extraordinary that words so simple could be conveyed so delicately, so musically. He wished to hear still other words. But evidently the harpist had finished. He had never raised his head, the head of a man perhaps thirty years old, the face earthen colored like Manco's own. Now the strumming of the harp was more resonant, Manco could hear it on every side of him.

The boy commenced to make his way back. He was neither tired nor cold. His chest was filled with the words the musician had spoken to him. The music, the same music which at first had unsettled him, now propelled him forward without strain, as if he were rainwater coursing down the face of a mountain to its source. But was its source in the river or the cloud? Manco smiled. "The mountain is born of the earth and brushes the sky." That was what the harpist said.

The next morning Manco awoke with a strange word on his lips. The word was "quena." It had not once, in his new life, entered Manco's mind until this moment. Immediately it entered his mind, the boy knew he must possess one. He must learn to play what he heard in the Altiplano, the tune of the mountains which the harpist called yaravi. Manco felt his cousin Pepito stir under the poncho. When the child turned to him he saw that Manco was smiling. Pepito looked at his cousin quizzically, then he smiled.

"I can hear a music, Pepito. It is called yaravi."

Pepito formed the syllables on his lips. "Yaravi," he repeated softly.

"It is here," Manco touched his chest. "It is here also," he touched Pepito's chest.

Pepito touched his chest. Then he placed his hand on his cousin's chest.

"You cannot hear it now, Pepito. But I will play it for you and then you will hear it also. I am certain that you will hear it as I do." After a pause Manco said, "I must go to the village today. There I can get that instrument which will enable you to hear what I hear within me."

"Yaravi," Pepito said carefully, as if in awe of the rich strange sound.

Now Manco's mind turned to the problem of getting to the village, called Oroya, which was fifteen kilometers to the west. It would be better to wait until market day when the farmers of the Altiplano carted their goods to Oroya for the mercado. But market day was still three days away and the urgency Manco felt made it impossible for him to wait. He must get to Oroya today lest the tune that sounded so clear within him fade.

By this time the household was fully aroused. His cousins were preparing for pasture.

Manco's oldest cousin addressed him: "Do you come with us, Cojito, or do you stay behind?"

"I am going to the village," Manco replied.

"To the village? For what reason do you wish to go to the village? And how do you expect to get to the village?"

"I will wait by the roadside and ask a ride of whoever is going in that direction."

"And if nobody is going in the direction of Oroya? What will you do then, my little Cojito? Will you walk to the village? Or perhaps you will run?"

Manco did not reply.

"Perhaps it is that Cojito has a novia in the village. Tell me, my little cousin, do you expect to find a little cojita in the village of Oroya?"

Manco's uncle called to his eldest son to make haste. As the cousins rode off, Pepito turned and smiled at Manco.

Manco quickly drank a bowl of maté de coca, then put on his poncho and hobbled outside. His aunt, who had been feeding the pigs and chickens, looked at him with surprise.

"Manco, where are you going?"

"I am going to the village." In order to avoid further questioning he explained how he meant to get there.

Aunt Soledad wiped her hands on her skirt. "Wait here. I will give you some food to take with you."

She went into the casita. In a few minutes she returned and handed Manco some food wrapped in newspaper. As

Manco was securing it in his poncho, his aunt brushed his head affectionately—then turned abruptly, scolding one of the pigs that had wandered too far. With one foot she nudged it back to the feeding trough, all the time scolding it, but with play in her voice.

Manco hobbled in the direction of the dirt road 200 meters due west of the casita. It was not until he was well under way that he realized how sore his body felt from the long journey he had taken the day before. The muscles of his shoulders and back especially felt sore. Yet he was not tired. Rather he felt as he had felt yesterday making his way back to the pasture area from the sierra, with the yaravi singing to him from every side of the Altiplano. Now too he heard the yaravi, he saw in his mind's eye the musician bent to his harp. And today there was something else, another sound similar to the harp, joined to it, yet thinner, pitched higher. The sound came from the wooden pipe called quena. At the mention of this word Manco felt a stirring in his chest that excited and unsettled him at the same time. At once he suppressed the sensation. Now he must concentrate on getting to the village of Oroya.

Manco paused at the dusty narrow road. The road was unpeopled as far as he could see in either direction. Except for a small flock of vicuña near the southern horizon, the Altiplano looked desolate. From where he stood Manco could not see the rock outcrop of the eastern sierra. He wondered whether the harpist was yet there. Manco looked up at the sky: only the briefest glimmer of sun was visible between the thick grey clouds. After several minutes Manco sat on the hard grass at the side of the road. He waited.

A few hours later Manco with his eyes closed, but awake, was still waiting. He opened his eyes and looked up. A large black vulture was circling high above him.

"Not yet, Condorito," Manco said to the bird. "It may not appear so to you, but I am just beginning."

Manco was surprised by his own words. He smiled, folded his poncho beneath his head, and lay on his side. He waited for perhaps another hour with his eyes open, then closed his eyes.

Dust settling on his face and in his nose and mouth awakened him. He heard the sound of an engine. A carro was coming along the road, but going in the opposite direction, towards him, away from the village. The yellow machine stopped in a flurry of dust beside Manco. A young man and an older man were inside. The young man at the controls was dressed in a poncho and chullo, but the older man was dressed strangely in a fabric the color of rain clouds and with shiny brass buttons. On his head he wore an oddly-shaped cap beneath which his hair was cropped like an alpaca. It was he who addressed Manco.

"What are you doing here by the side of the road?"

"I am waiting for someone who is going to the village of Oroya with whom I can get a ride."

The strange man looked Manco up and down. "What happened to your legs?"

This question, though it was not asked brutally, startled Manco. He did not know how to answer.

"Do you know who I am?" the strange man continued, removing his cap and displaying his cropped head and jutting ears. He was holding his cap out in front of him, pointing to the words which were engraved on it.

"Do you know how to read?"

Manco, who could read a little, could not read the words on the cap. Before he could reply, the man moved his finger slowly from word to word, pronouncing distinctly.

"Ejército de Salvación," he said loudly. And looking at Manco with an intense look, he repeated these words: "Ejército de Salvación."

Manco recognized that the words were in Spanish, but he did not know what they meant. But then the man spoke two Spanish words which Manco did recognize: "Jesús Cristo." The man stared at Manco. "Ejército de Salvación is the army of the Lord. And Jesús Cristo is the great general of this army," he explained in Quechua.

After a pause during which time the man continued to stare at Manco, he repeated the sentence exactly, then said: "You too can become a soldier in this army. The fact that you are legless is of no importance in the service of Christ."

Finally, perhaps growing tired of staring at Manco, the man put his cap on his head, touched the driver's wrist, and the carro departed discharging dust and smoke. Manco shielded his face with his poncho. When the dust and smoke cleared somewhat Manco looked in the direction of the machine until it faded beyond the horizon.

Without thought Manco commenced to hobble along the side of the road in the opposite direction.

After a time he heard the sound of hooves behind him. He stopped and waited until an Indio, a campesino riding a horse and leading a llama, passed alongside him. The man paused, then gestured with his head. Manco nodded and the man leaned to the side and hoisted Manco onto the horse behind him. He took Manco's crutches, fitted them on the llama's back, shook his reins and continued his deliberate trot in the direction of Oroya.

Manco looked back at the tethered llama. It was burdened with wood, much wood freshly cut and tied. Manco knew it was freshly cut because of the scent. It was wood from a cone forest. Manco knew of no cone forest in the Altiplano. Possibly it had come from the southern face of the sierra, which however was a great distance away.

Manco had many times ridden on the back of a llama, but he had never before ridden on a horse. The rhythm of the horse's movement was different. At first Manco held on to the poncho of the campesino, but the man adjusted Manco's hands so that they encircled his waist. That was better. Manco allowed his body to relax, to move easily in accord with the horse.

The campesino was not one who spoke with words. Manco recognized that at once, and welcomed it. He had had enough of words—Manco was thinking of the man with the cropped head and the brass buttons. The experience with this man had pained him. Especially since it had taken him by surprise. Still, the boy's thoughts continued, he should not have been so affected by it as he was. He had on several occasions seen other of his people who took on the customs of the "Cruces," the mixed breeds, who spoke with Spanish words, and who snapped their fingers at those Quechuas who refused to renounce their customs.

This man with the cropped head was no better nor worse than the others who believed as he did.

The campesino was a lean strong man. Manco felt the tight sinew of his waist, and he saw the thick tendons of his neck between his chullo and poncho. Manco focused on the man's back deliberately in order to keep his mind from returning to the man in the yellow carro.

For several hours Manco had forgotten about the quena, the yaravi. Now it came to him again. He felt good again.

After they had been traveling for a long while, the man stopped his horse and slipped down to urinate. Manco remembered the food in his poncho. He opened the package and took out a handful of grain and potatoes. He offered the package to the campesino who had gotten back on the horse.

"No. You will need it," the man said.

Manco folded the package and fitted it back in his poncho.

By the time they finally arrived at the outlying area of the village, the first star was showing in the sky, and Manco was feeling cold and tired. Oroya lay beneath them in a small valley. The campesino stopped at the top of the trail that wound down to the village. He slipped down from the horse, then lifted Manco down. He removed several twigs from the wood on the llama's back and commenced to prepare a fire.

"Sit here," he said to Manco, pointing to a stone at the side of the trail. He handed Manco his crutches.

After the campesino had prepared a small fire, he removed a tin pot from the llama's bundle and disappeared down the trail carrying a lighted splinter of cone wood. Listening, Manco heard the rippling of a small stream. The campesino reappeared a few minutes later, his pot filled with water from this stream. He placed the pot on the fire. When the water was boiled he sprinkled some coca leaves into it. Then he sat next to Manco. Manco felt the welcome heat of the fire, he listened to the boiling water and smelled the wood burning. It was a scent he knew and liked. He had smelled this same wood burning many times. It had been cut and gathered by his father in the cone forest high above the city of Cuzco. He had not smelled this scent since he had come to live on the Altiplano, because there llama or alpaca dung was burned as fuel. Nor had the image of his father entered his mind until this moment.

The campesino poured maté de coca into a small bowl, mixed a chunk of brown sugar in with it, and handed the bowl to Manco. Though it was very hot, it tasted so fine that Manco drank it rapidly. He handed the bowl back to the man, who poured the remainder of the maté into it, mixed in the sugar, and drank. But slowly, sipping the hot tea. As Manco watched him drink he felt the tenderness of his own scalded tongue and palate. He had drunk the tea too rapidly.

Though it was not more than an hour past sunset, Oroya appeared nearly deserted. A few persons on mule-back, two or three borrachos staggering through the streets, a man—a Cruce—with a big stomach and a large pistola on his hip leaning against a wall, smoking.

"I do not stop here," the campesino was saying to Manco. "Do you want the plaza?"

"Yes. The plaza."

The campesino stopped in front of a wide square section of dirt and grass with a statue in its center and broken stone benches scattered about. The campesino slipped down, lifted Manco onto the ground, then handed the boy his crutches. The man and the boy looked at each other, then the man removed his chullo and fitted it on Manco's head and over his ears.

"Hasta la próxima—until the next time, little friend," the man said as he got onto his horse.

Manco, less cold in the chullo, yet still cold and somewhat numbed, watched the campesino, the horse and the tethered llama loaded with cone wood make their way up a small rise, then down it and out of sight.

The boy looked about him, then hobbled into the plaza towards its center. Here a statue was raised above a stone fountain. The fountain was without water and the stone basin was chipped and littered with debris. The statue was intact. It was of a fierce man with an unsheathed sword on a rearing horse. Manco could not decipher the words on the pedestal but knew they were in the language of Spanish.

Manco touched his chullo with his hand. The fabric felt old and soft, as of the best alpaca. And his head felt warm and comfortable as if he had always worn it. He felt much gratitude to the campesino. The boy reached into his poncho and removed a handful of potatoes and grain. Chewing, he felt the irritation on his tongue and palate. He had drunk the campesino's maté too greedily. He would not make that mistake again.

Manco looked up at the sky which was clear and filled with stars. He could distinguish several clusters, the one called the Scythe, the one with the outspread "wings" that resembled a cóndor, and the cluster his people called the Humpback, which was also a portion of the cóndor. As often happened when he looked at the stars, Manco felt isolated in his stunted body. His haunches felt stiff and numbed from riding on the horse for so many hours. Manco wondered about the campesino. Where had he gathered the cone wood? Where was he going? Through his mind's eye Manco envisioned the cone forest above the city of Cuzco. Then he saw the blackish grey outcrop of rock of the Altiplano. And beneath it the musician bent over his harp. "Yaravi." Manco said the word aloud. Then again. The word was somehow separated from its music. Manco touched his hand to his chest but felt only the hollowness of bone beneath his poncho.

He heard someone. The Cruce with the big stomach and the pistola on his hip was speaking loudly and laughing. Manco, who did not want to be seen by this man, hobbled away from the noise into a narrow calle that intersected the plaza. The calle was dark, spotted with sewage ditches and broken stones. Using the light of the stars to make his way, Manco hobbled carefully and quietly. The calle led into a small dumping area. Manco could smell it, and he saw the rats moving in and around the debris. He turned to the left, then to the left again beyond the dumping area. Here he stopped. The Cruce would not find him here, though Manco could still hear his laughing from the other side of the plaza.

Manco touched the package in his poncho—the food was nearly gone. He was feeling cold. He did not know what he would do next. He turned around. Only after he had begun to hobble in the direction from where he came did he realize that he was heading for the dumping area. There he might find some kind of shelter until morning.

Ignoring the offensive smell Manco threaded his way through the clutter. The rats scurried on either side of him, though at a safe distance. The garbage was mostly the remains of food. But after a while Manco came upon something large and hard. It was wood and Manco could smell that it had been recently burned. Likely tomorrow or the next day it would be reclaimed for firewood. But tonight it would serve as shelter. Manco moved around the object, feeling it with his hands. It was too large to have been a door. It might have formed the front or back portion of a house. There was space enough for Manco to slide between the object and the ground. He did this, arranging his poncho beneath him. For a time Manco could hear the rats scurrying for food, then he fell into sleep.

When Manco awoke in the first light of dawn, his clothes and face were wet from the garúa-mist. At first he forgot where he was, but then he remembered. He crawled out of his covering and wiped his face with the inside of his poncho. The vapor rose out of his mouth and nose. Manco felt cold, his haunches felt sore. He looked at the large wooden ruin which had been his shelter. It was badly charred. Manco touched his hand to one of the charred areas and came away with some sticky residue. He recognized the scent of cone wood on his fingers. Examining the ruin more closely, Manco concluded that it was the back and side portion of a small house.

Manco could feel the sun now, though it was partially obscured by clouds. It felt good on his head. He thought he would go to the plaza where he could warm up a bit, then decide how to go about acquiring his quena. The prospect of acquiring one at all seemed much more remote than it did when he had spoken of it to Pepito only the day before. And the yaravi Manco had heard on the Altiplano was less heard than remembered now in the cold dawn in the dumping ground.

The boy was about to make his way out when he spotted a heap of debris and charred wood a few meters from the wooden ruin. He hobbled up to it, poking the pile with his crutch. It appeared that all or most of it came from the house Manco had slept beneath. Slivers of cone wood, some pottery shards, charred cardboard and newspaper. Reaching in for a page of newspaper to read the date, Manco was astonished to see that the newspaper was nearly four years old. Probing more deeply with his crutch, Manco uncovered broken glass, a portion of a spoon, more charred wood, and newspaper. Again he examined the newspaper: it was the same date as the other sheet. Now Manco was uncovering the debris with a purpose, moving his crutch carefully back and forth . . . Near the bottom of the pile he made contact with something that sounded like wood. He reached in with his hand and came away with a flute, a quena, painted red and yellow. Evidently intact. No, a small portion of its base was burned away. And a piece of charred newspaper was stuck to the mouthpiece. This Manco scratched off. He placed the quena to his mouth without touching the holes and produced a single unbroken note . . .

III THE MARKET PLACE

For the next several months Manco worked at learning how to play his quena. He worked at it tirelessly and at all hours, trying to produce with the instrument the music that was locked within his chest. This music, which the harpist had called yaravi, Manco often "heard" note by note, as distinctly as he had heard it that day on the Altiplano watching the bent man stroke his harp. Other times Manco did not clearly hear the music, and at first these times discouraged him. Yet he continued to practice, relying, when the yaravi was unheard, on echoes, on instinct. And always when afterwards at some point he again heard the yaravi, he discovered the notes he had been teaching himself to produce were the true notes.

During the first few months after returning from Oroya, Manco practiced in the casita exclusively. He did not go with the zagalejos into the campo. But after a time, having become more familiar with his quena, Manco did on occasion go with his cousins in the early morning. Pepito now sat behind Manco, holding him by the waist, steadying him, while Manco used his hands to play his instrument. Though Manco played far from well, Pepito listened as if enthralled. What Manco had felt with such assurance on that morning after his return from the sierra, seemed to be true: Pepito also had yaravi within him.

Manco's uncle and older cousins at first found the quena entertaining, but after a while they scarcely noticed it. With Aunt Soledad, it was different. Since Manco's return from Oroya her attitude had become more affectionate. Never a demonstrative person, she expressed her new feelings silently, in a gesture, with her eyes . . . Manco witnessed this alteration in his aunt and felt warmed by it.

In the campo Manco would sit on the grass and play his flute, listening to the thin notes emerge and circle in the vastness. Often he would glance at the dim grey outcrop of rock in the distant sierra, wondering whether the harpist was there. Manco was never tempted to see for himself. He knew that it was not yet time for him to return.

Sitting on the grass Manco sometimes looked up at the sky and at the low dark clouds in their subtle yet infinite shapes. When, as formerly, this vastness threatened to produce in him a feeling of dejection, of isolation and smallness, Manco thought of his quena, of the yaravi. And on the rare occasion when even these thoughts were not powerful enough to nullify his loneliness, he thought of the words the harpist had spoken.

"The mountain is born of the earth and brushes the sky."

Those were the words Manco kept within his chest, having uttered them only in moments of special need.

Manco and Pepito did not speak together more often than before, nor did they spend more time together, yet the bond between them was even closer than it had been. Once, soon after Manco had returned from the village of Oroya, Pepito awoke weeping in the middle of the night. Manco too awoke and turned to his cousin. Holding the boy's head in his hands with gentleness, Manco whispered softly into his ears until Pepito drifted peacefully back into sleep. Manco knew then what he had not seen earlier, that Pepito's chest not only contained yaravi, but the desert vastness which was yaravi's place.

A year had passed since Manco's return from the village of Oroya. In this time he had learned to play yaravi. He was now twelve years old and ready, he thought, to contribute earnings to his uncle's household, if not to make his way entirely on his own. Sunday was the market day in Oroya. Manco's idea was to arrive in Oroya on Saturday, find a spot in the market area where he would play his quena, then return to the Altiplano on the day after market with one of the campo families. Not only the campesinos and the village people of Oroya, but occasional travelers from other lands, would visit the market, hear Manco's music and perhaps give him a few centavos. After two days he might be fortunate enough to accumulate ten soles, not a large sum, yet enought to be of some use to his household.

Before notifying his uncle of his intentions, Manco decided to return to the sierra, hoping there to find the harpist. It was not until now that Manco felt ready to confront this experience. Even now he was not certain that he was ready, though he felt he must be, having learned to perform the yaravi.

The following morning he went with his cousins into the campo. Once in the grazing area, Manco separated himself and began the trek to the sierra. For some reason that he did not understand his body was responding poorly. He had hardly covered 200 meters when he became tired and had to rest on the ground. Manco removed his quena and looked at it. He placed it in his mouth and fingered the holes, though without blowing into it. He did not know what was wrong with him, why he felt not only tired, but restless and uneasy. In two days he would begin a new time in his life, playing yaravi, contributing to his family. For so long he had felt the shame of a parasite, taking food, shelter, yet giving nothing. Feeling the contempt of his cousins for his inability to work. Soon it would be different. He would do his share, or as much of his share as he could manage. And still he was uneasy, restless in his body. Manco did not understand it. He fitted the quena in his poncho and struggled up.

As on the first time Manco had gone to the sierra, this was the season of clouds and cold without rain. But today the wind was active, blowing from the northwest, rippling through the rough puna grass, unsettling the soil. Then ceasing. Then commencing again. Manco pulled his chullo more tightly over his head. In order to combat the fatigue that was taking hold of him, he hobbled more rapidly, holding his head against his chest to diminish the bite of the wind. He knew it would have been better to turn back, return another, calmer, day when he felt stronger. Instead he stubbornly pushed forward, having made up his mind to make this journey before starting for Oroya on the following day.

When the wind lessened Manco saw the outcrop of rock. He was not yet close enough to see whether the musician was there, seated beneath it. Once, while he rested, he detected the strains of a harp—which might also have been the murmur of the wind through the puna grass.

Manco was no more than 100 meters away. He did not see the harpist . . . No, the man was not there. Manco hobbled up to the rock. It appeared, the entire scene appeared, less vivid, less defined than the boy had remembered it. Beneath the shelter of the jutting rock was the very stone the harpist had sat on. Now Manco sat on it, laying his crutches on the ground beside him. His face, covered with dust, he wiped with the inside of his poncho. He removed his quena and commenced to play, bending to his pipe as the musician had bent over his harp . . . He stopped. The sound was thin, without richness. He straightened his back, put the pipe to his lips, and clearing his mind of thinking, played again. This time it was good, the austere and plaintive notes rising out of him without strain, circling into the wind. As he played, Manco opened his eyes, gazing calmly at the space surrounding him, which seemed neither desolate nor threatening. He closed his eyes.

When he awoke his flute was on his lap. Glancing at the piece of sun visible from behind the clouds, Manco supposed that he had slept for nearly two hours. In the distance near the western horizon he saw a llama which must have wandered from the others. For a time Manco watched its gentle, rhythmic gait.

Manco's uncle accepted without comment his nephew's decision to go to Oroya. Perhaps he was skeptical that Manco could earn any money. Or perhaps he was relieved that for nearly three days a week there would be one less mouth to feed. Pepito was saddened. Aunt Soledad smiled and said that she would give him something. Manco thought she meant she would pack some food for his journey, but as he was about to leave at dawn the following day, his aunt presented him with a small wooden charm in the shape of a llama.

"A llamita," she said. "For good luck." Then she gave Manco some food wrapped in newspaper.

Manco waited no more than an hour by the roadside before getting a ride in the back of a mule-drawn cart which was loaded with trussed-up piglets and the three children of a campo family. Manco played his quena for the children, though without concentration, having to listen to the squeals of the small pigs, who were to be sold and slaughtered.

Once in Oroya the cart stopped in front of the plaza, in and around which the mercado was being set up. Many of the sellers of livestock and hard goods had already arrived and were arranging their wares. The venders of perishable items such as fruit and vegetables and meat would be arriving later, closer to market time. Manco hobbled through the plaza away from the livestock area.

This was the first mercado he had been in since he had come from the city of Cuzco. Of course the Oroya market was not so large nor so varied as the market of Cuzco, yet the resemblance was there in the good-natured bustle of the venders, in the clutter, in the smells. This resemblance filled Manco's chest with warmth, though within this warmth was another, smaller, place that was hollow, desolate. Manco recognized this other as the feeling which had possessed him during his first years on the Altiplano. Then he thought of it as a coldness, as of ice. The music of the yaravi had penetrated this ice, as the sun of the Altiplano melts the snow on the peaks of the sierra. Yet not entirely: a desolate space windswept with memory remained. And when the yaravi was gone from him, as sometimes happened, all of him was memory . . .

Between the west side of the plaza and a small stall managed by an old man who sold copal, frankincense, and other incense materials, and facing the declining sun, Manco spread his poncho beneath him and sat on the ground. After he played a few notes on his quena, the incense vender turned to him.

"I have not seen you here before, Cojito. What is it you sell?"

"I am not a vender, Señor. I am a musician." Applied to himself, the last word sounded strange to Manco's ears. He played several more notes of the yaravi as if to prove both to himself and to the vender that he was a "musician."

"You sell your music then," the old man said.

These words surprised Manco. Put that way his intentions sounded without heart.

"How many soles do you think you will make selling this music of yours?"

"I don't know," Manco replied. "Whatever it is I earn will be more than I now have."

The modesty of this response appeared to impress the old man. "Where are you living then?"

"I am living on the Altiplano, southeast of Oroya."

"You stay with your people?"

"I stay with my uncle and his family."

"And where are your proper parents?"

"They are no longer living, Señor. With permission," Manco said, taking up his flute and playing.

The old man continued to look at the boy for a time, then turned back to his wares.

Although the mercado had not properly begun, a number of Oroya townspeople were buying at the stalls, and several dropped coins in Manco's cap. What surprised and a little saddened the boy was that not one of them appeared to listen to the music. Those who noticed him at all, saw a legless boy playing on a pipe. Either this was sufficient to inspire their charity, or it was not. The fact that Manco was playing yaravi with skill and heart made no impression.

But it was still early, the boy reasoned. Tonight and tomorrow there would be festivity in the air. People would be more disposed to listen, to share a little in the spirit of the music.

The weather continued agreeable into the evening, and Manco felt comfortable in the spot he had chosen to play his instrument. In the meantime the incense vender's wife joined her husband, noticed Manco, and began to ply him with questions. The boy responded politely, though briefly. The old woman gave him a bowl of maté.

It was wholly dark, with the waning moon directly overhead, when the people, many of them carrying straw baskets or woven bolsas, began to enter the mercado in earnest. Manco was playing more loudly now in order to be heard above the din. His chullo, containing ten or twelve coins, was fastened to one of his crutches which he had planted in the ground. Of the people who paused near his spot, most questioned Manco about his legs. When he mentioned earthquake, they sighed or gestured consolingly and dropped some coins in his cap. The coins were coming more readily than he had expected, but they had nothing to do with his music. Three times he started to play and each time he was interrupted so that he might answer questions about his legs. Finally he removed his poncho and draped it about his thighs.

Now when he played he was not interrupted. Many people stopped on their way to or from another stall, some listened for a moment, a few deposited a centavo in his cap. After two or three hours with his poncho on his stumps, Manco was feeling cold and somewhat dejected. It mattered less to him that he had not been doing well with his injury obscured, than that nobody appeared interested in his music. Could it be that yaravi, which to him was as important as life, meant nothing to the others? Could they continue to wear the ancient costumes, swallow the bruja's remedies, boast of the legendary beauty of Machupicchu—yet not respond to the very music that sang of this history, that sang of their long sorrow?

Manco removed the poncho from his stumps and put it on properly. He took up his quena and commenced to play—but was interrupted by the sound of chimes. The bells of the Iglesia had begun to chime loudly. Manco could

see the Iglesia from where he sat, it was the highest structure in the village. Even as the chimes were ringing, shoppers, pausing with their baskets, wished to know how
Manco had become cojo . . .

By the end of the night the boy felt as though he had
spoken more words than in the accumulated time he had
lived on the Altiplano. And for what reason? So that he
might beg a centavo. That is what it came to, people giving
a crippled beggar-boy charity.

The incense vender, closing his stall for the night,
peered at Manco who was still sitting on the ground with
his flute on his lap.

"Well, and did you make a lot of money, Cojito?" He
glanced into Manco's chullo. Then shook it. "You did very
well for your first time. There must be nearly fifteen soles in
this cap of yours."

Manco looked blankly at the old man.

"But why are you just sitting there? Do you not have a
place to sleep tonight?"

The incense vender's wife had come out of the stall.

"The cojito does not have a place to sleep tonight," the
old man informed his wife.

"The poor boy—"

"Not so poor," the old man grinned, shaking Manco's
cap. "He must have fifteen soles here."

"I must go now," Manco said, removing his chullo and
fitting it in his poncho.

"But won't you even count your money?"

"I will count it later," the boy answered, gathering his
crutches.

The old woman, who had gone into the stall, emerged
again with a blanket.

"You must not spend the night with just your poncho.
Take this cobija and return it to me tomorrow."

Manco accepted the cobija, thanked the old woman,
and began to make his way across the plaza. The grass and
benches were already occupied by market people who were
preparing to sleep. Manco hobbled away from them, in-
tending to spend the night in the dumping area as he had
the first time. But he was not able to locate it, first turning

down one wrong calle, then another. The din, the lights, and especially all the talking he did during this long day had wearied him. He stopped and looked around, trying to get his bearings. Though there were no lights where he was, Manco soon determined which direction he needed to take.

There was a change: the dumping area was now surmounted by a gate, the door of which was locked. Manco heard the sounds of the rats moving among the rubbish. It was too dark for him to see anything with clarity. Turning, he hobbled slowly back to the plaza, where he spent the night.

The following day, Sunday, was for Manco like the day that preceded it, but on a larger scale. More shoppers, more questions, more coins dropped into his chullo, less music. During the entire time only one person, an old beggar from the village, listened to Manco's music without either interrupting or moving away. Glancing at the old man's eyes as he played, Manco saw in them a brightness which resembled the glaze on the Altiplano grass after rain, beneath the strong sun. When he finished his tune the old man continued to gaze at him.

But then more shoppers surrounded Manco, and when they left so had the old beggar.

Early the following morning, as Manco was making his way through the plaza to the area from where the carts were departing, he passed beneath a small stone arch he had not seen before. In the center of the arch was the image of a face. Manco paused to look at the face more closely. It was triangular in shape, flattened at the head, with engraved lines surrounding it like a halo. But the most remarkable aspect of the face was that it was laughing. Struck by and impressed somehow with the image, Manco turned to a man who was passing and asked its significance.

"Ah, this is the Arco del Sol, my friend. It is muy anciano."

Afterwards, on the way back to the Altiplano, sitting in the same cart that had transported him to Oroya, without the pigs, Manco counted his earnings. Nearly twenty-three soles: much, much more than he could have expected.

That evening he presented the money to his uncle.

"How much do you have here?"

"Almost twenty-three soles, Uncle."

His uncle was surprised. "That is very good. It will be of help to us."

Manco felt pleased.

For the next year Manco continued to spend two or three days a week in the village of Oroya, playing his pipe for centavos in the market. Aside from the old beggar, whom the locals called "Tonto," meaning slow in thought, and whom Manco saw nearly every week for the first several months, nobody *heard* his yaravi. Yet in this year's time, Manco never returned to the Altiplano with less than twenty soles, and several times he returned with as much as twenty-five soles. Sorely disappointed at first with the lack of attention paid to his music, Manco grew to accept it. And as he played less and with less heart, he spoke more, with more facility, about himself, the loss of his legs, the earthquake in the city of Cuzco. And after a time these words became so familiar that he was capable of residing behind them, as it seemed, listening to them without partaking of them. The same replies to similar questions, his words spoken with the same inflexions, the same pauses. And Manco himself isolated behind them. Not only were there a small number of different people who attended the market each week, but many of the same people continued to pause by the crippled boy long enough to say a word and deposit a coin in his chullo.

Thus it continued. On one occasion Manco arrived in Oroya without his quena, having forgotten it. When he saw that it scarcely mattered, he left it at home more often. Among the market people, only Tonto, the old beggar, noticed the omission. After a time Manco ceased to see him.

Once, as the year was declining, Manco was returning to the Altiplano earlier than usual, hobbling from the road to the casita—when he heard notes being played on a quena, haltingly played. When Manco went into the house he saw that it was Pepito, who, squatting against a wall, was blowing into Manco's quena. Surprised, Pepito looked at his cousin, his eyes uncertain. Manco's initial response was more complex than joy—yet joy was what his nearly spontaneous smile conveyed.

"My little cousin has taken up the quena. Let me hear what you can do then, Pepito."

Smiling, Pepito put the quena to his lips, carefully attempting a yaravi . . .

"I am only just learning, Manco. I wish to play as you do."

"I am certain that you will do so. All you lack is practice. But why is it that you are not with the zagalejos?"

"Mamita is not well. Yesterday the sister stayed behind. Today it is myself."

Pepito went with his cousin into the kitchen where Aunt Soledad was lying on a pallet. Manco needed only to glance at her to know that she was seriously ill.

"It is in her stomach," Pepito said softly, arranging the poultice on her forehead.

Soledad opened her eyes. She reached out and took Manco's hand. Her small calloused hand was colder than Manco had ever remembered it. When he looked into his aunt's eyes, he saw there the same sheen he had seen in the eyes of the old beggar, Tonto. This was the first time he had seen such a light in his aunt's eyes. It was, he realized, a bond between them. With her other hand Soledad motioned weakly to Pepito; the boy took hold of her hand. The three of them remained that way for a time, silently. Then Soledad closed her eyes and the boys left her.

The next market Manco earned twenty-one soles, ten of which he spent on a quena for Pepito. He presented it to him on returning from Oroya.

Two days afterwards Aunt Soledad died quietly on her pallet. She was buried in a small cemetery only a kilometer south of that portion of sierra where Manco had heard the harpist. As they passed the sierra on the way back from the burial, Manco touched the llamita, the small charm his aunt had given to him the year before. Manco understood that his time in the casita on the Altiplano was ending. He would make his way north to Puno, which was closer to the city of Cuzco than Oroya, and larger.

In Puno Manco would again play his quena, whether or not people chose to listen to it.

IV   THE CIRCLE

A short time after Aunt Soledad's death, Manco made his farewells to his cousins and left the casita on the Altiplano for the last time. The dawn was just breaking. Pepito walked beside him carrying a few items wrapped in a blanket. They stopped at the side of the road. Manco intended to get a ride to Oroya, and from there to get another ride to Puno. Manco and Pepito waited together without speaking. Though saddened at having to separate from his cousin, Manco felt mostly its necessity. Pepito's sadness was unrelieved. He had, he confided to Manco, imagined the two of them sitting together, playing yaravi on their quenas. Manco said it might yet happen that the two of them would make music together. These words, meant to console, were uttered with a conviction that surprised Manco.

Pepito pointed down the road: someone was coming. A man riding a horse and leading a llama. Manco recognized the campesino who had taken him to Oroya for the first time two years before, and who had given him his chullo. Again his llama was carrying a load of cone wood.

The campesino stopped near where the boys were standing. He touched his hand to his chest in greeting.

"You remember me from the last time, Señor?" Manco asked.

The campesino laughed. Manco suddenly recalled the laughing image of the Arco del Sol in the plaza Oroya.

"It is possible you do not remember me," Manco said softly.

"Of course I remember you," the campesino said. "How could I forget my little friend? You are returning to Oroya?"

"I am going beyond Oroya to the city of Puno."

"I will be going in that direction," the man replied. "You can ride with me." He took the wrapped blanket from Pepito and fitted it on the llama.

The two boys embraced, then the campesino lifted Manco onto the horse and they started off. Manco turned and waved to his cousin.

As on that first occasion two years before, the campesino evidently had no intention of talking much with words. This was just as well, since Manco, filled with feeling, had little to say.

Everything seemed much as it had that first time. Manco holding the man across his hard waist, observing the thick tendons between his poncho and chullo. This chullo looked identical to the one he had given Manco, except that at the back between the intersecting circles that formed the main pattern, was a llama. Manco removed his own cap and looked at it: his too had the llama. Oddly, he had never noticed it before, this earth-brown llama between the earth-brown circles.

After a few hours the clouds thickened and it began to rain. Manco was hunching his body against the cold when the campesino said something to him over his shoulder.

"You must not fight it."

Manco did not understand.

"This is the season of rain and cold," the man said. "If you close your body against it you will feel not less cold, but more."

Manco did not respond. But after a few minutes he raised his chest and breathed deeply. Even as the rain came harder, Manco tried to resist his inclination to huddle away from it. The campesino sat straight-backed, holding the reins in one hand, just as he had when they had begun in the early sun.

These were the only words that passed between them for the several hours the rain continued. The llama ambled quietly behind, with its burden of cone wood.

Finally, just before twilight, the rain ceased and the declining sun moved in front of the dark clouds. Soon afterwards, while it was yet light, the campesino stopped and slid off his horse. This was precisely the spot where they had camped the first time, on the trail above the village of Oroya. He set Manco on the ground and handed him his crutches. Manco sat on a stone and watched the campesino prepare the fire. Then he removed his quena from his poncho and played a little, softly. The campesino had led the animals to grass, set a pot of water on the fire and sat down next to Manco. Manco played with his eyes closed, smelling the burning cone wood.

The man handed Manco a bowl of maté, then poured the remainder of the tea into a tin cup for himself. Both drank the strong sweet liquid slowly, sipping it.

The campesino removed Manco's blanket from the llama, laid some newspaper on the ground near the fire, and spread the blanket on top of it. He tethered the animals to a single rock, then, arranging his poncho beneath him, lay down near the fire.

Manco slept deeply and peacefully, warmly, in spite of the damp and cold. The campesino awoke him while it was still dark, an hour or more before dawn. Soon they were moving down the trail into Oroya. As they passed the familiar plaza Manco felt without looking about him the early stirring of the market. He had spent three days a week here for a year begging soles. Begging, speaking words without heart, bartering his music for what he could earn. He was glad it was over. In Puno he would play his music even if he made almost nothing as a result. He himself would need very little to live from day to day.

The man and the boy stopped again in the late morning, just before the rain, to eat potatoes and beans and oca, and to drink maté de coca. They stopped near a stream where the animals drank.

"We will be coming upon the Lago," the campesino said.

Manco looked at him.

"Lago Titicaca," the man said. "Soon you will see it."

"Ah. I passed this way once before," Manco said. "Years ago. After I was taken from the city of Cuzco."

"And now you will be passing it again," the campesino said, laughing.

Manco did not understand the meaning of the man's laughing, yet he felt good listening to it.

"Let us hear you play your music then," the campesino said.

Manco removed his quena and played. The music sounded richer, truer than it had sounded in a long while.

"Mountain darkening," the campesino said softly after Manco finished. "Lovely. As the sun dying on the Altiplano is lovely. Yet there is another music," he continued, looking closely at Manco, "very much like this one, but that it sings of the mountain's light."

These words surprised the boy. "The mountain's light?"

"The sun dying on the Altiplano must again rise, is that not so?"

"Yes."

"In a legend of our people it was Condorito, the great bird, who carried the sun aloft each dawn from its resting place in Lago Titicaca. And afterwards at the day's end Condorito gently replaced the sun in the water. This is not a different sun, but the same." The campesino paused. "Just so, this music of the sun rising is similar to the other. Yet it is different."

"What is it called? This music of the sun rising?"

"It is called wayno."

"Wayno," Manco repeated.

. . . The Lago shimmered beneath them in the dying sun as they made their way. As far as Manco could see was light, silver and blue and the color of fire. The great bird on outspread wings carried the fire, sinking silently out of sight. Manco smiled. The vastness of the water was astonishing. It was as if he were looking at the Altiplano sky—beneath him. Yet he did not feel fear. He did not experience the smallness and isolation he often felt staring at the sky. With his eyes he followed the line of water until it merged with the sky. He listened to the soft rhythmic clop of the horse, of the llama. Beyond the sound of the animals' hooves, as if connected to it, he heard the steady whispering of the Lago. Manco felt weightless, as if something of himself was outside himself with sun and sky, water . . .

Although Puno was no more than ten kilometers beyond the Lago to the northwest, it was already dark when the campesino set Manco down near the plaza.

"Hasta la próxima. Until the next time then, my friend," the campesino said, touching his hand to his chest.

"Goodbye," Manco said, watching the man and horse and llama recede slowly into the darkness.

Looking about him, Manco saw that the people walking in and about the plaza were dressed warmly, hunched in their ponchos, many with woolen rebozos about their necks. He himself did not feel cold. He hobbled through the plaza, pausing at the statue in its center, which, like the statue in the plaza Oroya, represented a fierce armored man on a rearing horse. Only instead of a sword, this man held a scroll containing Spanish words which Manco could not read.

Manco made his way to the top of a hill, where he paused, looking down at the city. In one area, north of the plaza, he saw a concentration of lights which must have belonged to the main thoroughfare where the shops and hotels would be. At once Manco started back down the hill in the direction of the lights.

The pocked stone and mud became smooth stone as Manco approached the lights. Carros were here, honking noisily, discharging smoke. In the space of no more than 100 meters, Manco saw three buildings that were taller than the Iglesia in Oroya. And people, most of them Cruces, or from other lands altogether, walked on every side of him. Many of these people stared at him with curiosity. Manco hobbled through the entire lighted area, which was shaped like a square and was perhaps half a kilometer in width. Beyond this square, in the dim, flickering lights that dotted the hills, the Quechuas lived.

After making his way to the margin of the lights, Manco turned and headed back to a space of sand which bordered one of the tall buildings. He had noticed other Indios squatting there, selling food and textiles. Manco quietly deposited himself between two venders, took out his quena, and began to play tentatively, somewhat in awe of the people, the carros. His sound was not good, hollow, too thin, unequal to the din all about him. Yet already some passersby had paused to look at him. One dropped a few centavos in his lap, then two others did the same.

Again Manco took up his quena, and this time managing largely to ignore the noise, his sound was better. And yet it did not much matter, since within he felt nothing. But then he remembered the "wayno," which the campesino said resembled yaravi, yet was different, singing of light rather than sadness. He must, he felt, somehow learn to perform this wayno—

The Indio food vendor was speaking to him, asking where Manco had come from.

"For some time I have lived on the Altiplano, south of the village of Oroya."

The man said that he himself came from a small village north of Cuzco. Manco did not say that he had been born in the city of Cuzco.

"This music you play," the man continued, "it is called yaravi, is it not?"

"Yes."

"It is fine music. I have heard another play it as you do, but on a harp."

"Where? Where have you heard this harpist?"

"Why here," the Indio said. "In Puno. He is a blind man, a wonderful musician. But I have not seen him here for many months."

Manco wondered whether this was the same harpist

he had heard on the Altiplano. He had not seen that his musician was blind. And yet he might have been, since he was bent to his harp in such a manner that Manco could not observe his eyes.

"What is the harpist's name?"

"His name is Inti," the Indio said.

"Inti."

"Yes. But as I said, I have not seen him here for a long time.

More passersby had meanwhile paused to look at the crippled boy. Manco took up his quena . . .

Most of the people did not wait to listen to the music, but stared for a moment, gave him a few coins, or did not—and continued on their way. Unlike the people of Oroya who questioned him, these Cruces, obviously more knowledgeable of worldly matters, seemed satisfied merely to stare and pass on. Which permitted Manco to play his flute.

The vender, observing, whispered to Manco: "The Cruces have fear."

Manco looked up at him.

"The Cruces do not wish to learn who they were for fear that they might discover who they are." The vender laughed. "The music of yaravi tells them more than they wish to know."

The facility of this formulation impressed Manco, even as the apparent truth of it saddened him.

"And did they—the Cruces—not listen to the harpist?" Manco wished to know.

"Inti? Ah, Inti knew how to impress the Cruces when he wanted to do so. He would merely play a popular tune to capture their attention. As one gives a dulce to a child. Then, when they were gathered about him, Inti would craftily lead from the popular, lighthearted tune to yaravi. And the Cruces would find themselves responding without knowing it." Grinning, the vender looked closely at Manco. "It is what is called stealth. We Indios cannot make ourselves felt except through stealth, Cojito."

Manco did not know what to make of this. The vender's description of the harpist's "craftiness" was not in

accord with Manco's recollection of him. Perhaps this Inti
was another musician. Yet Manco somehow believed he
was the same, the same musician bent over his harp, playing not to "impress" the Cruces—but to space, to the vast
blankness of the Altiplano.

Manco, who accumulated nearly four soles in the four
hours he spent in the lights, spent the night in the plaza.
The following morning before dawn he opened his eyes
with the single purpose of finding Inti. Again he made his
way to the top of the hill, and from there he moved up into
the steeper hills where the Quechuas lived. By mid-
morning he located the small area where the quena-makers
sat carving and painting the quenas. Each of the three men
Manco asked said he knew of the harpist, but none had any
idea where he might be found. One of them suggested that
Manco inquire of an old "chaki," or hill-farmer.

It took Manco the rest of the day to find the chaki, who
said that of course he knew Inti, but no, he did not know
where the harpist lived, nor did he know when Inti would
return to Puno.

Manco did not get back to the plaza until after sunset.
That evening he spent as he did the evening before, in the
lights, playing yaravi, displaying himself.

These evenings passed slowly into weeks. When the
weather became too cold to sleep in the plaza, Manco slept
in the hills, in the hut of the chaki for a sol a night. This
chaki, the same who was acquainted with the harpist, lived
with his llama and tended to his potatoes and maize, which
grew in terraced strips on the hill beneath his hut.

Though not unfriendly, the chaki scarcely spoke.
Once, a month or so after Manco had come to live in his
hut, he inquired of the boy: "What do you want with Inti?"

The bluntness of the question after a month of virtual
silence, took Manco aback.

"I saw him once on the Altiplano. He was playing his
harp. I would like to see him again."

In response the chaki grunted, and that was the end of it.

On the other hand, the Indio food vender with whom Manco shared a plot of sand in the lights, spoke a good deal and about many things. Often he expressed himself on the evils of the Cruces. Yet when they approached his stall Manco observed that the vender never failed to smile excessively. This, Manco supposed, was what the vender meant by "stealth." At first Manco thought he did not understand this term, but then he recalled his time in Oroya, how he "performed" in the market, displaying his stumps, responding in Spanish to the same questions, accumulating soles. And was he not doing the same here in the city of Puno? It was true that here he played his quena, but the money he received had little to do with his music. Once, for two consecutive days, Manco experimented as he had in Oroya, covering his legs with his poncho, merely playing his flute. In those two days the boy made less than a sol, whereas he usually averaged five soles a day. Was this not proof that Manco himself was crafty and acted with stealth?

This realization disgusted Manco, it was so far removed from what he had set out to do. So far removed from the music of yaravi that he played now with little heart.

After nearly a year of working every evening and most days in the thoroughfare of lights, Manco was again confronted by the chaki.

"You have not yet seen Inti?"

"No. Is he here?" Manco asked.

"No, Inti is not here. How does it go down there—in the lights? You play your quena?"

"I beg, I play." Manco shrugged.

"Go to the quena-makers. There you can play." Then the old man left the hut to tend to his maize.

Manco was used to receiving an occasional terse utterance from the chaki. On this occasion he had spoken at greater length but even more puzzlingly. Why had he brought up Inti?" And the quena-makers?"

The day was warm and Manco decided to take a different, longer, route to the thoroughfare in order to pass the quena-makers. This time not three, but two men were there, sitting together against an adobe wall, working on their instruments. One of them glanced up at Manco, nodded, then went back to his work, carving the mouthpiece of a quena.

"Do you play your quena?" Manco asked. "Or do you merely make it?"

The same man looked at him again. "Do you make your instrument, Cojito? Or do you merely play it?"

This response surprised Manco. But then he smiled. "I never thought of it that way. No, I cannot make a quena." He paused. "Perhaps I ought to learn."

The other quena-maker, a younger man, looked up at Manco and smiled.

"Do you mind if I watch?" Manco asked.

The older man motioned to Manco to sit down. Manco sat next to the younger man, sliding against the wall. The younger man was boring the thumb hole in the instrument with a small tool Manco had never seen before. Manco took out his own quena and examined the thumb hole in it. He watched the other man whittling and sanding the mouthpiece. He examined the mouthpiece of his own instrument. Not in all the years he had had this instrument, had he looked at it so closely. The older man used a common cutting knife, but used it with such dexterity that the hard wood might have been clay. Manco placed the mouthpiece of his quena to his lips, then touched his finger to the thumb hole. Carefully he blew into it . . .

Every morning for the next several days Manco spent with the quena-makers, observing closely as they carved and bore and sanded and painted. In this time only a few perfunctory words had been spoken, but on the last day of the week, as Manco took up his crutches to start for the thoroughfare, the older man said:

"We will not be here the next time. We will be in the cone forest gathering wood."

"Where is this cone forest?" Manco asked.

"It is beyond the sierra in the direction of the Lago."

"Can I go with you?"
"Yes. Be here at dawn, Cojito."

When the boy arrived at the quena-makers' spot the following day, the two men were already there sitting on a brown and white horse. A llama stood nearby.

The younger man who was sitting behind, helped Manco onto the llama.

"Can you ride?" he asked. "Or shall I hold the tether?"
"I can ride."

Slowly they made their way down the hill, past the plaza, in the direction whence Manco and the campesino had come the year before. After a time Manco felt the bright light of the sun on his face. Unable to remove his hand from the bridle to shade his eyes for fear of toppling from the llama, Manco continued without sight for several meters. When he raised his head he saw that it was the silver and green of the Lago that had blinded him: it was there, the vast basin of light shimmering beneath them.

The older man glanced back.

"Here we turn," he said.

Manco maneuvered the llama to the left down a narrow sandy trail which cut away from the Lago at a diagonal. After a few hundred meters the sand gave way to hard soil, patches of grass. They were entering the forest.

On the ground here and there were cones which had fallen from the trees. Long-tailed black birds pecked at the cones. Manco smelled the scent of the wood. The trees on every side of him were the same as those he had known in the hills above the city of Cuzco.

The two men had gotten down from the horse, but the older man motioned to Manco, who would not easily make his way in the rough terrain, to remain on the llama. Then, farther into the forest, the younger man lifted Manco down from the llama.

While the older man chopped with his axe, the younger used his machete on the branches, cutting, stripping away the needles. They worked carefully, steadily, without words. When the wood was cut and piled it was bound and hoisted onto the llama.

Manco, looking at the sky, thought it must be an hour or so past noon.

The younger man was preparing a fire.

"We will eat," the older one said to Manco, spreading newspaper on the ground.

The three of them sat near the fire and ate potatoes and quinoa, a dark cereal grain. They drank maté de coca.

They started back, the pile of freshly-cut cone wood lashed onto the llama, who gave no indication that he noticed the heavier load. Manco thought of Pepito, how he would hold Manco steady on the llama while Manco played his quena. Manco thought of his father, and then for the first time in many years his mind turned to his mother and two sisters. For many years he had kept from thinking of his family, but now they came to him unbidden, without pain. Manco thought of Aunt Soledad, her cold hands as she lay in the kitchen dying. The sheen in her eyes. The Lago was beneath them. The clouds were thickening.

The quena-makers, who were brothers, agreed to teach Manco their craft. Manco had never used his hands in this way, and he did not learn rapidly at first. But he worked hard, with concentration, and his teachers were, as it seemed to the boy, infinitely patient. And after a time Manco became familiar with the carving knife, the borer, the hard grainy sanding paper, the finely bristled paintbrush. He learned how to select those herbs growing in the hills, which when added to wood-tar and ink and water produced the paint. And he learned how to use the machete to cut and trim the cone wood.

Every morning Manco would sit and work with the quena-makers. Most afternoons and every evening he would spend below in the lights, playing his instrument, displaying himself, making enough soles to eat and sleep.

One morning, many months after he had begun his apprenticeship, Manco was sitting alone with Tana, the older brother. Manco had been working on a quena for some time. Now he was testing it, placing a finger over each hole in turn, blowing, listening to pitch. It was satisfactory, yet not quite right. Several times Manco tested the instrument—with the same results. He glanced at Tana, who handed him a long thin wire.

"It may be in the bore," Tana said.

Manco carefully threaded the wire through the bore, dislodging a tiny sliver of wood. When he tested the quena again it was right.

Tana touched him on the shoulder. "It is right, Cojito."

"Yes."

Bueno. Play then."

Manco played softly, smelling the freshness of the wood. He noticed with surprise that Tana also had begun to play. Aside from producing a note or two to test the tone of a finished instrument, Manco had never before heard the craftsman play. He put down his quena to listen, but Tana motioned to him to continue. Together they played yaravi, the music gently, fluidly merging, but then as the tune ended, Tana continued playing something which was not familiar to Manco, though he recognized many of the notes and phrases. The tune was lilting, joyous, one phrase leading to another, then back, then forward, round and round as in a dance.

"Wayno?" Manco asked as Tana put down his quena.

"Yes, wayno. Do you wish to learn?"

"Yes."

Tana smiled.

One evening Manco took his place in the lights and proceeded to play the wayno. Almost immediately several Cruces paused to listen. The wayno was so structured that it permitted endless embellishment, adding or diminishing as a stream would gliding down the face of a mountain. Manco continued in this manner for some time watching the Cruces shake their heads to the rhythm, smile; and then, almost imperceptibly decreasing the tempo, he merged into the plaintive yaravi . . . All of the listeners remained. A few perhaps even heard.

The food vender heard. His face looked surprised.

"When did you learn that tune, Cojito? I mean the first one you played."

"Recently. I have been practicing."

"You are a clever fellow. That is just how Inti went about it. Do you remember Inti, that harpist I told you about?"

"Yes."

"Well, he knew that these Cruces are like children, and he would feed them their dulce, play them their popular cinema tune. Merely to gain their attention, you see. And then when the Cruces were wholly unprepared, Inti would craftily lead into yaravi. How else, my little friend, can you get to their purse strings but through their flinty hearts! And now you too have learned the secret."

"It is not a cinema tune that I was playing," Manco said. "It is called wayno and it is a tune of our people, of the mountains, even as yaravi."

"Yes? Well, you may say so. Whatever you choose to call it, it is as sugar to flies. How much did the Cruces drop into your chullo? Go on, count it. You are on your way to becoming a rich man."

V SEED ON STONE

For the first time since he was a child in the city of Cuzco, Manco's life seemed ordered and Manco himself felt generally contented. He continued to work as a quena-maker, and though he was neither as dexterous nor as rapid a craftsman as Tana or his brother, Tana considered his quenas sufficiently well-made to sell to the tourist markets in the city of Cuzco. Once every other month Tana or his brother made the long trip to Cuzco, delivering their quenas to an outlet store, which then distributed them to smaller shops in the tourist circuit.

Manco had by now permanently moved into the hut of the chaki, but as before he spent nearly the entire day outside, working as a craftsman in the mornings, then proceeding to the lights where he played until late into the evening. Since learning the wayno with its numerous embellishments, Manco became more popular with the Cruces, and as a consequence he made more money, enough to put away two or three soles each week. The boy also continued to play yaravi, though naturally not so frequently as he had when it was the single tune he knew. And the powerful emotion that accompanied his playing when he first learned yaravi several years ago was no longer present.

One evening in the season of rain, as Manco was performing in the lights, two men, one old and the other younger, paused to look at him. Though both of these men were Quechuas, they wore white-man costumes with shiny brass buttons. Manco remembered: the older one was the very man in the yellow carro who had questioned him years ago as the boy was waiting by the roadside on the Altiplano. He stopped playing. Both men were now staring at his legs. Manco wondered whether they recognized him.

"You play with skill," the older man remarked in Spanish. He then said other words which Manco did not understand.

"You do not understand Spanish, do you?" the older one asked in Quechua.

"Only if the words are spoken slowly."

"Very well," the man continued, speaking slowly. "I said that you play your instrument with skill. Have you ever thought of performing in the service of El Señor?"

Manco did not respond.

"How did you lose your legs, Cojito?"

"In an accident."

"Accident? Life is a series of 'accidents' for those who live outside the bosom of El Señor." The man removed his cap: "Ejército de Salvación," he read aloud, pointing to the words engraved on the cap while looking hard at the boy. "This is the army of El Señor, and we are always seeking soldiers to become a part of this great army. That you are legless does not matter in the service of Christ, since every soldier does what he can do best. In your case you would perform on your flute." The man replaced his cap on his head. "Come to the Iglesia tomorrow morning at 8:30, unless"—here the man cocked his head and grinned— "you wish to lose an arm."

Manco stared at him.

"What I am saying," the man continued gravely, "is that to live as you are doing outside the bosom of El Señor, is to continue living a life filled with what you call accidents. That is what El Otro would like you to call them. Accidents." He examined Manco with intense eyes. "You have heard of El Otro?"

"The devil," Manco said.

"Exacto." The man turned his head and spit over his left shoulder. "We will expect you tomorrow. In the Iglesia. 8:30."

Manco, who usually arose at dawn, remained on his mat the next morning. He had tried to get up but could not. The stumps of his thighs were swollen and painful. Because the chaki had already left to tend to his crops, Manco could do nothing but remain on his back. He lay that way until sunset when the chaki returned.

"You are sick," the chaki said.

"I cannot walk."

"Does it pain you to lie as you are?"

"No."

"Then remain so. I will go for the woman."

The woman was an herb-seller and a curandera. In a short while the chaki returned with her.

After she looked at Manco's thighs, she said, "Both stumps are infected, especially the left. It is from the rain, the cold."

"It is bad?" the chaki asked.

"It is very bad."

"How then will I go to the lights?" Manco asked.

"You must not now think of the lights," the woman said. "You will remain here in the chaki's hut and take what herbs I give you. We must try to keep this infection from moving. I will return in a short time with a powder. Do not take any food or drink in the meantime."

When the woman left Manco said to the chaki: "I have never before been sick in this way. Not since the legs."

"It is tough luck, Cojito."

"I have accumulated soles."

"Do not trouble yourself about that now, Cojito."

The woman returned with her powder. Manco swallowed it, and then he slept.

Manco was alive, the infection had been arrested. Only now his stumps were useless. Every week Tana brought wood and Manco did his quena-making in the hut. In the afternoons when the weather was mild, the chaki carried Manco outside, where sitting beneath the hut, the boy looked out over the hills and played his quena.

Aside from the chaki, Tana, and the woman, none of whom could spend much time with the invalid, Manco's sole companion was the chaki's llama. It used to be that the chaki used the llama to transport his crops and to carry his tools, but since Manco's sickness he had begun to leave the llama behind on most days. At first the animal remained outdoors while Manco worked or played his flute. But after several months, when Manco's stumps, though useless for hobbling, were somewhat healed, the chaki suggested that the boy occasionally ride the llama. Manco was not certain whether once mounted he would be able to stay put without the use of his thighs.

"You will hold with your arms," the chaki said. He lifted the boy onto the llama's back.

Subsequently Manco learned how to mount the animal without the aid of the chaki. First he slid from the mat to the door, where the llama, waiting, would bend its neck far enough for the boy to grab hold and swing himself onto his back. The chaki had contrived a bridle out of rope, which Manco used to maintain his balance and to steer.

The more adept Manco became, the farther away from the hut he ventured. He did not, naturally, hazard the steep hills which led down into the plaza. Nor did he return to the thoroughfare of lights. But he became a familiar figure in the Indio quarter in the outer hills of the city. The children, when they saw in the distance the queer outline of the cripple atop his llama ambling in their direction, would point and shout and cheer.

Once, one of them who must have seen Manco in the lights, shouted:

"Play your quena, Cojo!"

The other children took up the shout, running round and around the llama.

"Play your quena, Cojo!"

When Manco returned the next afternoon he was prepared.

"Play your quena, Cojo!" the children shouted.

Manco stopped, removed his quena from his poncho and began to play, holding on to the bridle with one hand. He needed but one hand to play certain variations on the wayno.

The children were suprised and delighted by the lilting music.

The adults too found Manco's presence comforting, greeting him heartily, plying him with food and drink. And if Manco did not return for a few days, they felt—or pretended to feel—that he was neglecting them, and they scolded him jestingly.

Manco thought it most strange that he whose luck had not been good, had become a "huaca," a symbol of good fortune, for others. Nor did he understand how this had come about. Which is not to say that the adulation displeased him. It warmed him even as it mystified him. Yet why was it that even in the midst of this adulation Manco felt remote, small; the sensation he experienced when he used to stare at the sky above the Altiplano? The isolation was not so intense now as it had been then, but it was similar in kind. It felt natural and good when he played wayno for the children who danced about him singing and shouting, stroking the llama. It was with their parents that he became uneasy. They gave Manco food or flowers, more and more often they touched his stumps for luck, they chatted a bit—and then they closed their doors and went back to their families, to their lives. The fact was—and Manco came to this only after considering it for a long time—they lost sight of Manco the human in their adulation of Cojo the huaca.

"Why," Manco asked the chaki one day, "do the Indios feel that I bring them good luck?"

The chaki appeared surprised—or surprised that Manco could make such an observation. But then he said: "They feel your power."

"What kind of power?"

"Power to—" the chaki paused, seeking the right word "—to continue."

Manco looked at him.

"You have survived the great earthquake. You have lived on the Altiplano. You have played your quena in Oroya, and now in the city of Puno. You have become a fine quena-maker. You have been further crippled and nearly killed by an infection. But you have learned to ride with the use of your arms. And to play your quena with a single hand."

These words seemed incredible. "But do the Indios know all this?"

"They know what they know," the chaki replied.

. . . The seasons continued, fading into, out of each other. Manco, who for several years had not felt like a boy, was in fact no longer a boy. Of the people he knew, one, Tana's brother, had died when the footbridge he was crossing on the way to the city of Cuzco collapsed. As a consequence, Manco, whose skill in making quenas steadily improved, worked more hours a day at his craft. He did most of the work in the hut, though on occasion he rode his llama to the quena-makers' area where Tana would lift him off the animal, and the two would work together as they had when Manco first arrived in Puno. Since his brother's death Tana spoke even less than formerly, but this did not matter to Manco. The two men enjoyed working side by side.

The chaki, though now a man of many years, still tended to his crops, but with the help of a young boy whose name was Tampu.

As before, Manco spent his afternoons and some of his evenings in the hills, playing his quena, chatting with the people. The adulation with which the people formerly greeted Manco's arrival, remained, but was tempered and perhaps dulled a little by familiarity. Which for Manco was just as well.

Also in the hills were the borrachos, the Indio men, and boys too, who begged or borrowed or perhaps even stole enough soles every few days to get drunk on chicha. Manco saw them in the hills and down below as well, sprawled in the gutters, wailing in their pain. People merely stepped around them. These, the tormented ones, were the ones Manco wanted to reach with his music. But they did not hear him.

Manco sometimes thought of the people of his earlier years, especially his father, and Aunt Soledad, and Pepito. The young boy, Tampu, who helped the chaki, reminded Manco of Pepito. Tampu was also fascinated with the quena, and Manco taught him how to play the wayno with certain of its embellishments. These days Manco seldom played yaravi.

Towards the end of the fifth winter in Puno, Raymi appeared. Raymi was a young woman who lived in the hills. She surprised Manco one day as he was sitting beneath the hut playing his quena. After he finished she came right up to him and introduced herself.

Manco was about to say his own name, when Raymi said: "I know you. Everybody does, you know."

"Oh."

"And I have heard you play before too, but never this. What is the name of this music?"

"Yaravi."

"It is very beautiful. And it is very sad. Is that why you do not play it, because it is sad?"

Manco did not know how to answer.

"I have heard it before, this yaravi," Raymi continued. "But never the way you played it."

"Perhaps that is because I have practiced," Manco said. "There was a time when I worked very hard at this music trying to master it."

"Did you succeed? Did you succeed in mastering it?"

"No," Manco said simply.

"It may be that you succeeded better than you think. Will you play it again?"

Manco looked more closely at the attractive young woman. "I do not think so. Not right now, Raymi."

"When then? When will you play it again? Will you play yaravi tomorrow if I come here?"

After a pause Manco said, "Yes. If it means so much to you I will play it again. Tomorrow."

"Very good," Raymi said. "I will come tomorrow at just this time. To listen."

The young woman came the next day and Manco played for her. They spoke for a while, and then she left. The day after she came again and the same pattern was repeated. Raymi returned for six consecutive days to listen to Manco's music, to talk. And then on the seventh day she failed to come.

Her absence unsettled Manco. That night he slept fitfully, thinking of her. Her presence, her voice, her energy—everything about her engendered an energy in himself he had never before experienced. Raymi did not return for five more days, and Manco thought it likely he would not see her again. But then she came.

"Hola, Manco."

"Oh, Raymi. You've come."

"Yes. Did you expect me not to?"

"I didn't know."

"I had to go to the village of Tacna. That is why you did not see me."

"I see."

"Yes. I have people there. But now I am here. Will you play yaravi for me?"

"Yes."

Manco took up his quena and immediately he blew into it he knew he was playing yaravi in the old way. He closed his eyes. Not in many years had it sounded so right, had the plaintive notes unfolded so naturally.

When Manco opened his eyes Raymi was smiling at him.

"Sometimes you close your eyes when you play, other

times you do not," she said. "What do you see when you close your eyes?"

Manco considered this. "It is not always the same. Just now I saw the Altiplano, a portion of the Altiplano that I had visited as a boy."

"The Altiplano is desert, is it not?"

"Yes. Desert and sky and space. It is very vast."

"But that sounds so lonely. Do you not ever imagine people when you play yaravi? To me your music speaks of—love." She looked at Manco, her eyes mischievous. "Did you learn of love on the Altiplano?"

This question embarrassed Manco a little. He did not respond.

"Will you do me a special favor, Manco?"

"Yes."

"Tomorrow when I come to you and you close your eyes to play yaravi, think of me." Raymi's eyes had a light in them. "I must go now," she said.

Manco knew that the sensation he felt was not love merely, but bodily love; and that the light in Raymi's eyes was the light of passion. Though awed by this new sensation in his bones, Manco was sufficiently clear-headed to worry about its outcome. What did Raymi expect of him? If it was passion she wanted, would he, a cripple, who had never before touched a woman in that way, be able to supply it?

The next day Raymi returned, and Manco played yaravi for her. But when he closed his eyes he could not see her image clearly. The yaravi itself, skillfully enough played, was not as it had been the day before. Manco wondered whether Raymi would notice the difference.

"Well, and what did you see?" she asked coyly.

"I saw you, Raymi."

"And was that better than imagining the Altiplano? Or not so good?"

"How did it sound to you?"

"It sounded as if you were more at home in your desert," she answered mockingly. Then she laughed. "It may very well be a lovely desert. I should like to see it."

Manco smiled.

"You are a strange man," Raymi said.

"I?"

"Yes. You are a quena-maker, a musician. Some people think you are a magician as well."

"Magician? I do not know what that means."

"What is it that you know? What is it that you wish to know?" Raymi asked in a serious voice.

For a moment Manco did not respond. Then he said: "I do not know what it is I wish to know. It used to be that I wished to know something of the nature of life. I thought that I might discover this through my music. There were a few times, brief times, when I even thought I made such a discovery, and that I would be able to share it with others. But then it left me. And since then I have become older, less ambitious. I have also become this," Manco pointed to his stumps. "It is limiting, you see," he smiled ironically.

"One forgets that about you. Your legs."

These words were naturally spoken, and very kind. Manco felt grateful.

Raymi was about to say more—but stopped herself. She left, and she did not return the following day. Nor the day after that. But then she returned, three days after her last visit. She came earlier than usual. Manco was sitting on his mat, sanding a flute. He looked up and their eyes came together naturally, like water flowing into water. They embraced, she held his head tenderly to her breast, they made love gently, passionately . . .

As she was about to leave, Raymi turned to Manco: "And what do you think of love now?" she smiled.

Manco thought of that question, of "love," all that night. He wished to prepare an "answer" for Raymi when he saw her the next morning. By the time morning came, Manco had not come up with anything he could put into words. The words that might do justice to the richness, the luxury, of this new sensation, he did not possess. He took up his quena—but neither yaravi nor wayno seemed at all adequate. Neither even brushed his new feeling.

When the appointed time came, Raymi had not arrived. But of course there was no appointed time with

Raymi. It was possible that she might not come at all today. Nor tomorrow. Had this sequence not been enacted before? But before there had not been love. There had not been what they felt lying on the mat in each other's arms.

Raymi did not come that day. She had not come for five days when Manco sent the boy, Tampu, to try to find her. When Tampu returned he told Manco that it was said that Raymi went to the city of Cuzco. It was not known when she would return.

For the next several weeks Manco was spiritless, working without concentration, sleeping badly, often neglecting to ride through the Indio quarter in the afternoons. When it was again time for Tana to travel to Cuzco to deliver the quenas, Manco asked to go with him.

"It is a difficult ride, Cojo."

"Yes. I will take the chaki's llama."

Manco had no idea how he would proceed to look for Raymi once he got to the city of Cuzco. He took a few provisions. The next morning Tana on his old brown and white mare, the bundle of quenas lashed to his saddle, was waiting for him.

Once above Puno they made their way to a mountain trail that followed the curve of the sierra twenty kilometers, after which they had to go down-mountain to pick up another trail which would ultimately lead to a dirt road on the outskirts of the city of Cuzco.

Manco, riding behind Tana, brushed the llama's head affectionately: "This will be a hard one, llamita."

Once on the trail Tana got off his horse and lashed Manco's thighs to the llama. The trail was dry and mostly clear of rock.

It remained clear for three or four kilometers. Then they turned into their first "slide." Tana shoveled rock and sand against the mountain, then led the llama through the narrow opening. This was repeated several times for the next five kilometers, and then the trail widened.

"I am sorry, Tana," Manco said.

Tana glanced behind him questioningly.

"I am sorry I am useless at this."

"Do not be sorry," Tana said.

The trail was now proceeding up-mountain and nar-

rowing. Once, twisting up and around, they startled a
vulture from its perch. It flapped away without a sound,
gliding to another peak across the canyon.

"Condorito," Manco said.

"Yes," Tana smiled.

The next slide was a large one, it covered the entire
trail.

"Better to turn back for a kilometer into the mountain.
Go around this," Tana said, slipping down from his horse.

The first leg of the journey to Cuzco continued in this
way, in and around slides, Tana shoveling, leading the
animals, Manco lashed like a totem to the llama, the llama
sure-footed, imperturbable.

It was just after sunset when they approached the
most difficult portion, the five kilometers steeply curving
down-mountain.

"We stop here," Tana said, already unfastening the
rope about Manco's thighs, "until it is light again."

Manco watched Tana prepare a fire and boil the water
for maté. Tana worked quietly and rapidly, with the same
economy of gesture with which he carved a quena, or rode
his horse.

Sipping the hot sugary tea, Manco thought of the campesino with whom he had traveled to Oroya, and then to
Puno. It was odd how much like Tana he appeared, often
merging with him in Manco's mind. He thought of Raymi.
It was of course possible that she had had to leave for Cuzco
so suddenly as not to be able to send word to Manco. But
this was not likely. Could it have been that the intimacy
they exchanged was of no importance to her? Could love
have been of no importance? Her eyes had indicated otherwise. The sheen in her eyes. But then Manco was a cripple.
In spite of how she said he "seemed," he was a cripple.
Perhaps it was this realization which, coming after their
intimacy, drove her away. For how could she consider
spending her life with such a creature? Manco had long ago
resigned himself to the kind of life that was possible for
him. But then the encounter with Raymi awakened just
those feelings which he thought were forever forbidden to

him. And then she disappeared, leaving him with this new surging in his body—and the grating awareness that he was but half a man.

Tana, squatting on the ground next to Manco, spread a newspaper of beans and quinoa in front of them . . .

Raymi had called him "strange," but really she was the strange one. Why else would she have come to him in the first place? Or having come, she might have found satisfaction in his music and gone no further. Manco stopped himself. This was selfishness. He was thinking selfishly in his pain. In his anger. It had been so long since he had felt anything that resembled anger. When the man in the brass buttons questioned him in the lights of Puno—that was the last time. Nearly five years ago. And now he was feeling anger towards the single person who loved him, who touched him, loving him. Raymi would be astonished to see him in Cuzco. He smiled.

The next morning, after Tana lashed Manco to the llama, he fastened a rope to the llama's bridle which he tied to the back of his saddle.

"This way is better," Tana said. "Very narrow here." He tapped the llama on the rump, then got on his horse.

Manco felt his body pushing against the rope as they started down-mountain. The grade became steeper rapidly, the pace painstaking; they picked their way down. After 100 meters or so Tana slid off his horse so that he could keep the animals close to the mountain on the extremely narrow path.

Several times Manco saw condoritos perched beneath them, peering into the mountain's cavity. The birds did not appear quite so commanding when glimpsed from above.

The sun was rising behind the riders, and then, as they twisted around the mountain, it was blazing fiercely in their faces. Tana stopped; from beneath his saddle he removed some newspaper which he dexterously worked into a kind of visor. He slipped the visor beneath Manco's chullo. Then he fashioned one for himself.

At a point perhaps halfway down they came to the footbridge. This, Manco knew, was where Tana's brother had gone down. Since then the bridge was rebuilt. It was about ten meters across and a meter and a half wide, with a rope railing on one side. Beneath was the space of the canyon.

"We will move the animals one at a time," Tana said. He unfastened the llama's bridle and walked the horse across the bridge. Then he returned and led the llama across.

They camped outside Cuzco. The following morning they rode into the city Manco had left nearly fifteen years before. It seemed strange to him, for he had lived in the hills of Cuzco. He had no recollection of ever having been below where they were now, making their way to the outlet store to deliver their quenas.

Manco saw an airplane cut diagonally above them as they rode. He remembered that once in the lights of Puno he had overheard two Cruces speaking of the new "aeropuerto" in the city of Cuzco. It was true.

In the distance to the east Manco saw the towers of two Iglesias side by side. Then as they were turning up a broad calle he saw yet another Iglesia to the northwest. Ahead were tall buildings, many containing large shops which had not yet opened, it being only a few hours past dawn. Manco assumed that this was the section of the lights where the Cruces and the tourists gathered. His eyes traveled to the mountains above the city: there he himself had lived with his family . . . Tana was turning up a calle to the left. He stopped, slid off his horse, and undid the bundle of quenas. A Cruce, standing in the entrance of a store, strode forward.

"There's Tana. You are just in time, Tana," the Cruce said loudly in Spanish. "The Gringos have already arrived, you know. They buy, they go to Machupicchu, they leave," he laughed. "But especially they buy, so these flutes of yours have come just in time."

The Cruce now turned to Manco. "You are the cojo, are you not? I must tell you, my little friend, that your workmanship is first class. Believe it or not, some of the Gringos can tell the difference in these things. They refuse to buy the flutes from *them*," he gestured to the mountains.

"Our Cuzco pobres are not good craftsmen. They would much rather sit on their asses and drink chicha." He shrugged his shoulders. "They get borracho, we get the soles. Which is not so bad, eh, my friends?"

Tana followed the Cruce into the store, returning in a while with soles in his hand. He gave them to Manco.

"Your share, Cojo."

Manco slipped the money inside his poncho.

"When do you start back to Puno?" Manco asked.

"In the dawn. For the animals it is too soon to start before."

"Yes. Then we will meet tomorrow at dawn. Where is best?"

"In the Plaza de Armas," Tana said. "Where the two great Iglesias are. Let us go there now."

More people were in the streets now. Also carros and colectivos—busses. People paused to stare at Manco.

The Plaza de Armas was much broader than the main plaza of Puno, and much more beautiful. The high brown towers of the Iglesias side by side blended with the red-brown of the hills and with the brown snow-tipped mountains beyond. Clouds and cloud-mist were everywhere, high and low, even in their path. Manco gazed up through the early sun at the sky which appeared to brush the farthermost mountains.

"I go to the hills. Do you wish to remain here, Cojo?"

"Yes."

"Until tomorrow then."

Manco watched Tana ride away. The plaza and the area around it were filling with people . . . Someone was speaking to him. Two Gringos were pointing to the llama and addressing him in a language he could not understand. A Cruce sitting on a bench nearby said in Spanish, "They ask whether they can snap a photo of the llama."

Manco looked at him.

The Cruce came over. "These are Norteamericanos. They would like to snap a photo of the llama."

One of the Gringos spoke.

"They will give you five soles if they can snap their photo," the Cruce explained.

Manco did not respond.

More people had come over.

"Well, can they snap their photo?" the Cruce wanted to know. "I'm sure you can use the money, Cojito."

"Yes, let them," Manco said.

The Cruce, nodding, spoke words to the Gringos, and the woman backed up slowly with her camera raised—but then lowered it. She said something.

"She wants to snap the photo by the fountain," the Cruce explained.

Manco glanced at the fountain in the center of the plaza.

The Gringa said something else.

"La Señora says she will give you seven soles to snap the photo by the fountain."

The Gringo husband spoke. Then the woman again.

"They will give you seven soles," the Cruce explained, "if they can snap *two* photos, one here and one near the fountain."

Manco was thinking of Raymi . . .

"Yes, it is all right," he said to the Cruce.

The Gringa snapped her photo. Then Manco started for the fountain, followed by a group of people.

The Cruce arranged the llama in front of the statue according to the Gringa's instructions and she snapped her photo.

Manco was moving away from the fountain when the husband overtook him and handed him seven soles. Seven soles were more than Manco usually earned for an entire day in the lights of Puno.

Several children were running after him, touching the llama. One Cruce child wanted to know the animal's name.

"Llamita," Manco said.

"Llamita, llamita . . . " the children repeated.

Outside the plaza Manco turned up a narrow calle. After he rode to the end of the street he stopped. He had no idea how even to begin to look for Raymi. Certainly it was hopeless to seek her here below, near the plaza, in the midst of Cruces and Gringos who had never before seen a llama. He looked above him at the hills.

Manco rode slowly in the direction of the hills, thread-
ing his way between carros, colectivos, trucks, people. So
many machines making so much noise he had not witnessed since his begging in the lights of Puno. And to the
llama it was entirely new, yet the llama moved through it all
as calmly as if he were still in the hills of Puno. Manco
thought of the hills of Puno. Then his mind moved to the
Altiplano: he recalled sitting on the small stone beneath the
outcrop of rock, playing his quena as Inti had played his
harp. When he had first come upon Inti, it seemed to
Manco exceedingly strange that he would be playing with
such intense passion to nothing. To the space and sky of the
Altiplano. It was not strange. Playing in the lights of Puno,
or (as he imagined it) in the main plaza of Cuzco, with
Cruces and Gringos staring, asking questions, snapping
photos—that was strange.

A large truck passed heavily very close to Manco—and
suddenly he recalled the tremor, the shuddering echo . . .
He wondered whether any of his people had survived.
Aside from his father and, less clearly, his mother, he had
no real recollection of any individual. Yet this was where it
had happened, somewhere in the hills of Cuzco, where he
was going now.

Two Indios were gesturing to him.

"You are going in the wrong direction, compadre,"
one of them said. "The procession is in the Quechua Plaza.
Turn to the right there, then to the right again."

Manco followed their instructions. Even before he
came to the plaza, he heard the solemn drumbeats. Pres-
ently he saw Indios, hundreds pressed together in the
small plaza. Manco drew closer but could not see above the
crowd. Something was happening in the innermost circle.
The drumbeats were loud, irregularly spaced. The people,
gazing intently, were silent.

"What is it?" Manco whispered to an old woman
standing in front of him.

"It is the Procession of the Lord of the Earthquakes,"
the woman replied.

Manco moved around the edge of the circle until he
found a vantage point from where he could just make out

the image of a dark figure on a tall pole. It was moving erratically in a circular motion. The pole was mounted on the shoulders of a Sinchi, or priest, who was supported on either side by a lesser Sinchi. The Sinchis were dancing, almost stalking, with intense exaggerated movements of their legs, slowly round and round in the circle. After several minutes of this, the dancing and the drumbeats suddenly ceased. People, one by one, were making their way into the inner circle, offering homage, and departing. After a time Manco's view became unobstructed. The dark image on the pole must have represented the Lord of the Earthquakes, and each time an Indio kneeled and placed an offering in the wooden casket draped with flowers, the "Lord" acknowledged the homage by inclining slightly forward.

Not every Indio chose to take part in the ceremony, though most did, and it was not until past mid-day, that the offerings were completed and the plaza nearly emptied. Now the drumbeats began again, joined by quenas, kanchi sipas, or pan-pipes, and a harp; and the Sinchis, followed by the musicians and perhaps fifty Indios, made their way out of the plaza. Of the musicians, the drummer and the flutists were young men, but the harpist was much older, and blind. Inti. It was him. Manco on his llama joined the procession.

Slowly it wound its way through the narrow walled calles, up into the hills, people and children and dogs joining or departing from the procession en route. Then, high above the city, the music, which had been mostly drumbeats and solemn adornments, gave way to ya-ravi . . .

The terminus of the procession was a large partially destroyed Iglesia. A portion of one of its towers had collapsed, and there were a great many fractures and chips in the stone facade. The Sinchis carrying the image mounted the steps, turned to the people, made acknowledgement, then entered the Iglesia. The music stopped, most of the people dispersed. The procession was over.

The harpist meanwhile had sat on the ground near the steps and begun again to play. Several people stood about, listening. Manco rode quietly up to them, got down from the llama, and slid next to the harpist. When the harpist heard the notes of the quena he nodded his head just slightly. The two of them played wayno, the phrases circling out brightly, then in again, out, the circle becoming richer within itself, and wider. The harpist led from one embellishment to another, each structurally related to the ones that preceded it. Manco followed easily, confidently, even as the embellishments became increasingly complex. He smelled the copal burning within the church—the scent was taken up by the music, as a blossom might by a stream weaving down-mountain. The group that was listening grew larger, more animated . . .

The pitch was now lower, the tempo slower. Manco was prepared when the harpist eased the wayno out of itself into yaravi, plaintive, austere, the thin-sounding quena shaping, containing the strings, the harp lending resonance to the flute. Manco opened his eyes: the harpist was bent over his harp.

They played until the sun set.

"You have come back," the harpist said without raising his head.

"Yes," Manco said.

The next day at dawn Manco and Inti, the harpist, were waiting in the Plaza de Armas when Tana arrived.

"Good morning, Tana," Inti said.

"Good morning, friend Inti."

"Tana, I have decided to remain in Cuzco," Manco said.

Tana did not appear surprised.

"Inti and I will play music," Manco explained.

"I am happy for you, Cojo," Tana smiled.

"Here I have some money that I owe to the chaki for the use of his hut," Manco said. "And as to the quena-making, Tana, I hope you will not think I speak out of turn when I suggest that you take on Tampu, the chaki's boy. He is, as you know, an aspiring musician who would like to learn as much as he can about his quena. I am certain he can become a good craftsman."

Tana nodded.

Manco was preparing to dismount, when Tana stopped him.

"You keep the llama, Cojo."

"But he belongs to the chaki."

"Listen to me," Tana said. "The chaki will be happy when he hears that you and Inti are playing together, and that his old llama will make it easier for you to get about."

Manco looked at Inti, then at Tana. "I will do as you suggest, Tana. Please thank the chaki for his kindness to me."

"I will, my friend. Now I will say farewell to you both." Tana touched his hand to his chest.

VI   DOS INDIOS

It was the season of sun and moderate cold without rain, when Manco had arrived with Tana in the city of Cuzco. Since then this most amiable of seasons had come and gone three times, and Manco and Inti were yet together, living in a small hut in the hills, playing their music. During this time Manco related to the harpist much that had happened in his life since the great shaking of the earth in the hills of Cuzco many years before. When he explained something of his love for Raymi, Inti said: "Seed may take root at once, or it may fall upon stone only to root long afterwards."

Of his own manner of living, Inti said little other than that he moved from place to place playing his harp.

"Do you prefer playing in the city of Cuzco to the Altiplano, Inti?"

The harpist did not respond immediately. But then he said, "In this respect I resemble our old llama, Cojito. Every place is to me both different and the same. When I am at the harp the differences vanish."

"And when you are not at the harp?"

Inti laughed softly. "When am I not at the harp, my friend?"

75

Once, after returning to their hut from an afternoon in the Plaza de Armas, Manco was in an irritated mood.

"Of what use is it to play to these Cruces, Inti? And to the Gringos? They snap photos, they ask questions, but they do not hear the music."

"A few do, in their own ways, hear, Cojito. Others who merely listen, may very well hear later. And if they do not hear, they do not."

"I understand what you are saying, my friend. I wish I might feel as you do."

"That large plaza where we played today, where we have played for so many days, because it is the most famous and visited area in all of Cuzco. What is it called?"

Manco was puzzled by the question. "Plaza de Armas, of course."

"Yes, Plaza de Armas. That is the name the conquistadores gave to it. But before they came it was known by the Quechua name of Wakaypata, which means Platform of Prayer. When I am playing in the plaza I do not feel I am in a place of arms, of weapons, but that I am in a sacred place of worship. Wakaypata."

"Times have changed, Inti."

"That is so, my friend. We now have an airport in the city of Cuzco. It is even possible that some day an Indio from this city will pilot one of the large planes that lands at this airport. Because, as you say, the times change. But does *time* change? Are we not now watching the sun slip behind the sierra, even as tomorrow we will see it rise above the sierra to the east? Has it not always been so?"

"Yes."

"Yes, Cojito. To live, not in the times, but in time, is to say 'yes' to Gringos, to Cruces. To airports."

Manco had not forgotten Raymi. Often, after not thinking of her for many months, her image would suddenly appear to him in a dream. Or he would imagine seeing her within a crowd of people in the Plaza de Armas. Though these rare moments were unsettling, the complex of feelings that had attended them when Manco first returned to Cuzco were now largely muted. The passage of time and Manco's satisfaction with his present life had combined to mute them.

Most mornings at dawn the two musicians would leave their hut, mount the llama and make their way to the Quechua Plaza in the hills. Here they would play and talk a little with their people. On occasion another musician would join in on his quena, or kanchi sipa, or on the drum. These times were good for Manco. The music, the comradeship with people he knew and with whom he felt at peace, were good. And yet satisfactory as this was, he was not entirely pleased. He missed the—he was not certain what to call it—exultation, that extraordinary sensation he had experienced when he heard Inti playing on the Altiplano, and that he had felt in his own playing on a few rare occasions afterwards.

"It was," he described the sensation to Inti, "as if a songbird locked in my chest had been set free."

"And now?" Inti asked.

"Now I cannot hear it within me, and so I cannot release it."

Inti did not speak.

"It is beyond my understanding," Manco said. "I had been certain that when I heard your music again it would release in me a—a like music. And now, for some years, I have heard your music daily, and never without the deepest admiration, my friend. I play with you in fact, as I had for the longest time in my imaginings. And we play well together. Especially in the estimation of those who listen to us, we play very well. And yet, Inti, I must confess that I feel I have failed you."

"Why do you feel such a responsibility to me, Cojito?"

"Because I have always considered you my teacher."

"I merely encouraged you to express what was already within you, my friend."

"What is it then? Why do I have this constant gnawing in me?"

"Let us go to the Iglesia in the hills, Cojito."

"To the Iglesia? Now?"

"Yes, now."

When they arrived at the Iglesia, the same church,

partially destroyed by the earthquake, that Manco had followed the procession to three years before, Inti helped Manco from the llama. They made their way up the steps.

"The door to the Iglesia is closed, is it not?"

Manco said it was.

"Look at the door closely, Cojito. Tell me what is engraved on it."

"As you wish. It is a scene of the Crucifixion. Jesús Cristo on the cross is being tormented by the soldiers."

"Who is this Jesús Cristo?" Inti asked.

"Who is he? He is the king of the Cruces and the Gringos, my friend. Who else can he be?"

"You did not listen, Cojito. I did not ask you who Jesús Cristo is, but who *this* Jesús Cristo is, the one that is carved on the door of the Iglesia."

Manco examined the Christ that was carved on the door.

"He does not look like any Cristo I have ever seen, Inti. His skin is dusky. His nose is the nose of a hawk. He looks like a Quechua."

"And the soldiers who are tormenting this Quechua? Describe them."

"The soldiers," Manco said, looking very closely at the frieze, "wear cascos on their heads. Their skin is white and they wear pointed beards and mustaches—" He paused.

"And their swords?" Inti asked.

"Their swords are shaped like the cross. They look like conquistadores, Inti."

"Yes."

"But what does it mean?"

"It means, Cojito, that the Indios who were forced to create this panel to celebrate their victimizers' god, did as they were told, having no choice. And yet at the same time, and within these limitations, they did as they must."

"And the conquistadores never observed this?"

"If they had," Inti said, "the door would not be standing today. Yet it would not have mattered if they had."

"It would not have mattered?"

"No, my friend. What mattered was that these great Indio craftsmen created what was, as you put it, gnawing within them. They knew that certain of their compadres would see it. But what was primary was not who recognized it, but that they expressed it." Inti paused. "Sit next to me on the steps, Cojito. This constant gnawing you have within you, my friend, is a result of your imprisonment in the particular circumstances of your life. These circumstances include the death of your family and what has happened to your legs. But it is this same imprisonment which has enabled you to sing of the freedom that was taken from you. You must learn to be like these wonderful Indio craftsmen and not take heed of who will or will not witness your creation. Your calling is to sing not only beyond the crippling of your body, but out of it."

Inti instructed Manco in the gathering of herbs, and once every twelfth day they would make their way up to the farthermost hills of the city, just below the cone forest. Here, on either side of the sandy trail, Inti would tell Manco what to look for and Manco, using his machete or his hands, would select herbs and moss and resinous bark. And sometimes they would enter the cone forest to gather a certain shrub-wood which Inti called palo de vida. Back at the hut the herbs would be spread on the dirt floor or outside under the sun to cure. Afterwards they would be combined according to their properties and used as powders or poultices. Like the curandera who treated the infection in Manco's thighs, Inti used his herbs with assurance. Once their old llama, who for so many years had loyally served first the chaki, then them, developed ulcers on his flank so that the slightest pressure from Inti's foot became unbearable. Inti combined four herbs and applied poultices to the llama's flank for three days. On the fourth day the ulcers had become calloused enough for the llama to suffer riders. By the seventh day the ulcers had disappeared altogether.

"Where did you gain this knowledge of herbs, Inti?"

"From another, my friend, even as you are learning something of it from me."

"And when you were on the Altiplano—did you gather herbs there as well?"

"There as well, Cojito. The grasses and wild flowers, the moss on the stones, all contain healing properties."

"I did not know that."

"It is so. Even we Indios have learned to rely on others, herb-sellers, curanderas, brujas, to supply our needs. It is cheap enough to purchase a bolsa full of coca leaves for fifteen centavos. Why then gather the leaves yourself?"

"Why then, Inti?"

"For the same reason that you became a quena-maker, my friend. Because the earth is alive and we are living upon it."

The Plaza de Armas was rarely empty, and especially in the "tourist season" it was crowded with people. Yet Inti was always as composed as the llama who deposited them near the fountain, next to the statue of the Castellano on his iron horse. Manco worked hard to attain a like calm, and on occasion he was successful, weaving his wayno, his yaravi, in and above and under the perfect phrasings of Inti's harp.

One afternoon as Manco was playing with concentration, he became slowly aware of a competing sound which appeared to grow louder as it became more sustained. Opening his eyes he was startled to see a large number of Cruces massed together in the western end of the plaza. A young Cruce was addressing them through a "bullhorn" in Spanish. Manco, with his eyes on the crowd, began to play perfunctorily, and then stopped altogether.

The young Cruce was shouting political phrases, a few of which Manco recognized as having seen scratched on the walls of public buildings. And sometimes a particular phrase would set the listeners to clapping their hands. Once the young Cruce shouted: "We must free our Indio brothers!" and the listeners clapped their hands. Yet the listeners did not, so far as Manco could see, include a single Indio. The Indios in the plaza were either washing in the fountain, or transporting heavy bundles on their backs. Some were listening to Inti's harp.

Manco noticed that a number of Cruce policía had entered the plaza from different directions. They made their way deliberately, in small clusters, all with pistolas on their hips, some carrying rifles with unsheathed knives at the tips.

And now Cruce schoolgirls were walking and skipping through the plaza in their blue uniforms, their books against their breasts, chatting loudly, giggling.

Several Gringos had meanwhile joined the Cruces who were listening to the bullhorn, and a few of the Gringos were snapping photos.

Indio venders walked among the crowd selling tamales and soft drinks. A few were displaying textiles to Gringos.

The young Cruce was shouting into the bullhorn with increased urgency, apparently in defiance of the policía, repeating the slogans, his voice breaking.

Manco looked up at the Iglesia towers, sheathed in cloud. His eyes followed the clouds to the red-brown hills and beyond to the purple-brown mountains tipped with ice. The ice reflected the sun. The sky was still.

After a time the speaker stopped shouting and the crowd slowly dispersed. It was becoming very hot and no one wished to remain in the sun. Some of the Cruces and Gringos paused for a moment to listen to the blind harpist and legless flutist play music. The Cruces gave centavos; the Gringos gave centavos and soles and some snapped photos.

When they returned to the hut Manco remarked to his friend: "The young Cruce was shouting about revolution and the Cruces listening were clapping their hands."

Inti nodded.

"The young Cruce shouted also about our people. He said, 'we must free our Indio brothers.' But the Indios were not listening."

"They have heard this shouting before."

"The young Cruce did not sound dishonest," Manco said.

"That may be, Cojito. But our people have heard the shouting of honest orators before."

"What is it then? Does all the shouting, all the passion, amount to nothing?"

"I am merely a blind Indio, my friend. And not a Cruce politician. But it seems to me that an orator, whichever side he takes, must orate. Whether results follow is another matter. As for our people, they know that the Castellanos who rule even the Cruces still feel as their ancestors, the conquistadores, felt, that this is their land under Jesús Cristo, and that the Indios belong in the mountains with their chickens and pigs and llamas."

"That is not just, Inti."

"No, it is not just. And yet there are different degrees of justness."

"I do not understand."

"These Castellanos under Cristo can have no idea how close to the spirit of their own God their Indio prisoners have become. And I do not refer only to the Indio craftsmen who designed the Iglesia door."

"With respect, Inti. I cannot understand how an Indio beggar has drawn close to the spirit of the Castellano's God."

"Perhaps then our perceptions of this matter are different, my friend. Yet perceptions change, and it is possible that our own may grow closer."

It was in the season of rain and cold, during the Indios' fifth year together, when, Manco alone in the hut, received a visitor. It was Pepito, Manco's cousin. They embraced warmly.

"You remembered me, Manco."

"At once. How could I not? How are my cousins on the Altiplano?"

"Things continue as usual. Except that Papá is getting old and cannot work as he did formerly. Which means that I cannot with conscience leave."

"You do not wish to remain on the Altiplano, Pepito?"

Pepito shook his head no. "Do you remember that you gave me a quena just before you left for the city of Puno?"

"Yes, I remember."

"I learned to play it, Manco. I learned to play yaravi."

"Pepito removed the quena from his poncho. Manco recognized that it was the very one he had bought in Oroya.

"Do you wish to join me?" Pepito asked softly.

"Yes."

They played yaravi together, Pepito playing sweetly and with refinement. He had taught himself well.

"It is good," Manco said. "It is a good music you make, my cousin."

Just then Inti returned.

"My cousin, Pepito, whom I have not seen in many years, is here," Manco explained. "He has come from the Altiplano. He wishes to become a musician."

"Ah," Inti smiled. "What is your instrument?"

"The quena."

"And do you have your quena with you?"

"Yes."

"Let us play then. The three of us."

"You say you wish to become a musician," Inti said softly after they had played. "You are already a musician, my friend."

Pepito smiled. "With respect, Señor, I am merely a zagalejo."

Inti bent over his harp and commenced to play again, yaravi. This time his phrasing was more austere, and the intervals between notes and phrases were longer, unevenly spaced. The effect was somewhat dissonant, but controlled. Manco had not until now realized how flexible the yaravi was.

When Inti had finished Manco commented on the "intervals."

Inti nodded. "That is the space of the Altiplano. I know that you have heard it also, Pepito. Now you must keep it within."

One morning Manco decided not to stop with Inti at the Quechua Plaza, but to continue farther up into the hills. Although he had no specific destination in mind, he knew that he was trying to get back. Increasingly Manco had been thinking of his childhood in the hills of Cuzco. Lately too he had been dreaming of his childhood, vague dreams redolent of cone wood, of children's voices . . .

Manco rode into the mercado area, pausing to watch

the quena-makers, two old men who worked methodically, silently.

"With permission, Señores, is the name 'Tupac,' familiar to you?" Tupac was Manco's family name.

Neither of the two men knew of it.

Manco then stopped in front of a very old woman herb-seller. At first she thought she knew the name, but when Manco explained that his father had been a woodcutter, she said she was mistaken.

Manco inquired of still other ancianos, none of whom knew of the family Tupac.

Meanwhile several children who recognized Manco, were following him, demanding that he play for them. Manco did, and as he heard the sprightly phrases of the wayno, the old pleasure of playing for the children in the hills of Puno came back to him. The children wanted to know why the blind harpist was not with him.

"Are you not brothers?" one of them asked.

Manco laughed. "We are not brothers in the strict sense, my little friend. We are compadres."

"Play another song, Señor Cojo."

Manco on his llama played, the children dancing and jumping about him.

When, afterwards, he joined Inti in the plaza, the harpist said, "It has been a good morning for you?"

Manco smiled. "It has, my friend."

"Yes. I can hear in your quena that it has been a good morning."

Manco, whose vivid, yet undefined, dreams of his childhood continued, continued his occasional journeys into the hills in search of any information regarding Tupac the woodcutter. Nearly every journey concluded with him performing for the children in the calles.

"These occasions when I have gone into the hills," Manco confided to the harpist, "I have been searching for someone, anyone, who knows something of my family."

"I see."

"I have found no one."

Inti did not speak.

"And you, my friend," Manco continued. "We have played together and lived together for several years now, and yet I know nothing of your background, your childhood."

"What do you wish to know, Cojito?"

"Whatever you wish to say. Have you yourself not told me that my early years have been in large part responsible for what I am today? And for what I may yet become? I am then naturally curious about your own earliest years."

"Unlike you," Inti said, "I was not disabled in an accident. I was born without eyes, so that I have always witnessed what I witness today. In that respect, my friend, I am still and will remain always a child."

Tana still made his periodic trips into Cuzco to sell his quenas. And always he would spend a few hours with the two musicians. On his most recent trip Tana had brought Tampu, the chaki's boy, who was now Tana's apprentice. After exchanging warm greetings, the four musicians played together. Manco was impressed with Tampu's increasing skill on the quena, and told him so.

"I thank you very much, Señor Cojo. I have had good teachers."

"How is the chaki?" Manco enquired.

"The chaki has died, Señor Cojo. I was planning on telling you. The chaki died peacefully."

"He was a very old man," Manco said softly. He was saddened. "And what has become of the chaki's hut, and his vegetables?

"The chaki's hut has been purchased by the woman Raymi. And her son."

Manco could not believe what he had heard. "Raymi, whom I had known, Tampu?"

"Yes."

"And her son?" Manco said weakly. "How old is her son, then?"

"I do not know precisely. I would say seven or eight years."

Manco could not question further.

After a few moments Tana said, "We must go, my friends. We will see you again."

As the two quena-makers were leaving, Manco forced himself to ask Tampu: "The boy's name? Do you know his name?"

"He is called, "Yaravi," Señor Cojo."

Tampu's revelation had unleashed so many varying feelings in Manco, that for the next several weeks he was listless and preoccupied. He still was not certain that he heard what he had heard: she was back and living with their child in the very hut in which the child had been conceived. And she had named the child Yaravi! How could it be? And where had she been all this time? Why had she not returned to him? Whether or not she had any feelings for him, surely she had an obligation to notify him, the father, of his son's birth. But how could she not have feelings for him: moving into his hut, calling the child Yaravi? Ah, Raymi. Manco wished he had asked Tampu more questions. What was her work? Was she tending to the chaki's crops? Who were her friends? And the boy—his son? Perhaps Tampu might have told him something of his son. Yaravi. So Raymi had not forgotten. She had not lost her love for him. Manco remembered again, vividly, the passion in her eyes. He remembered in his body their lovemaking . . . But then she left, and Manco had at last satisfied himself that she had left out of contempt, or disgust, or at the very least out of lack of love. But now she was back, churning in him the old brief tenderness, the old sorrow—all that he had accounted for as dead, now rekindled. To what end? Was she not capable of disappearing again? Was not this the manner in which she lived her life? The term "llorona" swept into Manco's head. A llorona was a woman-spirit who lived in the night. Once she embraced you it was death, because she was wedded to El Otro, the devil. Manco felt himself shudder.

Inti of course was witness to his friend's preoccupation, but he did not allude to it. In the Quechua Plaza, in the

Plaza de Armas below, in their hut in the hills, Inti continued as before.

Manco tormented himself in silence. His initial inclination to see Raymi—and his son—he had abandoned. And whenever a feeling connected with Raymi surfaced, he would strive to suppress it.

One morning, gathering herbs high in the hills near the cone forest, Inti said: "Next to the high grass away from this path there are several small clusters of green and purple weeds, are there not, Cojito?"

"Yes, I see them."

"We will take one of these clusters, but make certain that you cut out the entire root."

"What is this weed called, Inti."

"Alma."

"Alma? That is an odd name for such a common-looking weed."

"The name is apt, my friend. If used properly, alma will open the top of your head."

"What do you mean by properly?"

"I mean with respect. With respect for what you called its commonness."

Manco was trying to understand.

"Next we will go into the cone forest to cut some palo de vida," Inti said. "When the palo de vida is added to the fire its scent will mingle with the fragrance of the tea."

Back in the hut, Inti immediately began to separate and prepare the weed. Manco built a small fire on the hearth.

"Do not add the palo de vida until the fire is going well," Inti said.

Inti placed two pots on the fire, one containing the alma, and a smaller pot of manzanilla.

"I said that if used correctly alma will open the top of your head. If not used correctly it will also open the top of your head, but with great violence. That is why we burn the palo de vida, and why we are boiling manzanilla, my friend. Manzanilla is a close sister to alma, for it grows in the same soil. But whereas alma is bitter and powerful, manzanilla is, as you know, sabrosa, very delicate. It will make the tea more palatable."

In a while Manco was able to smell the strong acrid scent of the alma. Only after the peculiar scent had become very distinct, did Inti carefully add the manzanilla to the larger pot. As the combined herbs simmered, the aroma became sweeter.

"Drink slowly, with small sips," Inti cautioned.

The tea was strong and rich, with a certain latent bitterness to it.

"We will each take one more cup. Be careful not to spill any of the tea on the floor, Cojito."

Inti and Manco both were sitting on the earthen floor, facing the sunset through the open door. For a long time neither of them spoke.

"Remove your chullo," Inti said softly.

Manco laughed. "I am not wearing my chullo."

Inti was silent.

Putting his hand to his head, Manco discovered that he *was* wearing his chullo. As soon as he removed it he felt a freshness, as of a soft wind rustling through his hair. He had not realized how constricting the chullo was. He felt much lighter without it. Without it he felt, as it seemed, *clearer*. He could see effortlessly. Through the open door he saw the sun dying, and through the gold rain of its dying he saw a child and a man walking towards the cone forest in the direction of the rising sun. The father was speaking softly, his voice mingling with the garúa-mist and bird calls of the forest. These calls became louder—and suddenly so loud that the child broke away into the trees to escape from them . . . A man's head on a child's body blowing sweetly in a desert. The desert light danced slowly between sand and mountain and the wind made a spacious sound. The boy blew into his wood. The man touched the boy's stumps, saying: take this chullo, sing of it while wearing it, and when the seasons change, forget to remember me. The campesino touched his hand to his chest and Soledad was gone. Sun slanting on the shaking earth. An Indio at dawn beneath a rock, Pepito, smiling shyly. Tampu said: Raymi left you loving you, she gave you Yaravi. Ride your llama into the mountains, sing to the children of your legs gone, gold in the sun. The clouds ride slowly, fluidly, from west to east, and back again, touching, not touching, unceasing . . .

The following morning the two Indios were riding on the llama to the Quechua Plaza.

"I feel very well this morning, Inti."

"Yes? I am glad to hear it."

"Why, my friend, if I may ask this, did you choose to administer the alma only now, after all our years together?"

"The alma made the choice, Cojito. I merely recognized that the choice had been made."

Manco considered this. "I am afraid that I am a slow learner."

"Speed or lack of speed is of no real importance, my friend."

"Perhaps not," Manco said thoughtfully. "In any case I feel alive this morning."

"Yes. And we will let our friends in the plaza warm themselves in your music," Inti chuckled.

As time went on the two musicians became increasingly well-known, not only among the Indios in the hills and the Cruces below, but among the Gringos as well. Those Gringos who visited and listened to them, returned to their own countries and sometimes remembered to tell their acquaintances, who, when they came to the city of Cuzco, listened (if they remembered) to the musicians and were either impressed or not. If not, they would say: "These two old crippled Indians whom people talk about and even call saintly. I saw them, you know—and heard them play, and I assure you they are merely two crippled Indians playing a pipe and a broken harp for centavos."

Among those Gringos who were impressed, several took it upon themselves to visit the musicians in their hut. A few who could not speak Spanish even came with Cruce interpreters. At first these visits unsettled Manco, but he learned to accept them, or at least to accept their inevitability. Inti of course continued as always.

On one occasion, after two young Germans and their Cruce had left, Manco said: "What was it? I did not understand what they wanted."

"They wanted us to make money. And," Inti smiled, "to make some money from us."

"Is that what they meant by 'sponsor'?"

"I believe it is, Cojito. They want to 'sponsor' us. To fly us to their country."

"Fly?"

"Yes, my friend. From the airport of Cuzco. Would you like to fly in an airplane?"

"I would like to fly without an airplane."

They both laughed.

"That happens sometimes when you play, Cojito. Flying without an airplane."

"Yes. Sometimes."

Manco was surprised to discover that even among the Gringos there were some who actually *heard* their music. Manco could tell by their faces that this was so. A few of those who truly heard were themselves musicians, and they asked questions about technical matters. But since the questions were asked in Spanish, neither Inti nor Manco could readily discuss these things.

One Norteamericano who was adept at playing the iron flute of his country, wished to learn how to play the quena, and Manco agreed to teach him. The young Gringo's name was Ricardo, and when he visited Manco in his hut he was modest and quiet in his manner. He knew but a few phrases of Spanish so that very little talk passed between them. Manco would demonstrate certain fingerings and notes on the quena, and Ricardo would practice them. And when he was not practicing he sat quietly on the floor beneath the window and listened to the two musicians talk or play.

Even as Ricardo was learning the wayno with its embellishments, he expressed an interest in the structure of the quena. After some thought Manco gave him Tana's name when Ricardo was preparing to leave the country in order to renew his papers.

When Tana came to Cuzco some time afterwards, he

mentioned that the young Gringo was in Puno learning to make quenas.

"Does he make progress, Tana?"

"Yes, he does well."

"I am glad to hear it. And Tampu?"

"Tampu sends his respects to you and Inti. He has remained in Puno to continue the work, which is greater than before. The supplier told me only today that it is yourself who is responsible, Cojito. You are well-known in Cuzco."

"The supplier must be very happy," Manco said.

"He is very nervous," Tana said. "The more soles he makes, the more nervous he appears."

The Indios laughed.

Making their way up to the small plaza one morning, Manco heard the familiar moaning of an Indio who had spent the night in the gutter.

They stopped and Inti moved the man out of the road, propping him against the mud and brick wall of a hut.

On the llama again, Manco said: "That is one who cannot hear our music."

Inti did not respond.

"The Gringos listen to our music and buy quenas that make the Cruce businessmen money. While the Indios lie drunk, moaning in the gutter."

"You say that the Cruce businessmen are not in their own ways drunk, my friend?"

Manco considered this.

"Yes, in a way they are also drunk, I suppose. But they do not suffer so much, so undeservedly."

"I cannot speak of 'much'," Inti said. "There is great suffering everywhere. Perhaps it is all undeserved."

"Perhaps," Manco repeated with some irritation. "What then do we do?"

Inti did not respond immediately. For a few minutes they rode in silence.

"We do," Inti repeated finally, "what we can. We play music to those who will listen, and our music matters to those who can hear. When one of our people is drunk we move him away from the road."

"And then we continue with our music," Manco said ironically.

"Then we continue with our music," Inti said. "That purple and green weed called alma grows out of our dead compadres' chests. If you had violently pulled it from the earth and drunk it angrily. What then?"

"I would not have witnessed," Manco said softly.

"No, you would not have witnessed. And without witness you would not have continued your music. Not truly."

After a pause, Manco said: "You have spoken in this manner before, Inti. And yet it is difficult for me to remember."

"It is never not difficult, my friend."

That morning in the plaza Manco was recognized. A very old woman who watched him closely while he played, finally asked whether he was the son of Tupac.

"Yes, Tupac," Manco said excitedly. "Tupac the woodcutter. You knew my family?"

"Yes, I knew. My family too perished in the great terremoto. I alone survived." She gazed at Manco through eyes that had long since accepted the tragedy.

"I heard that the son had survived, but broken. And also a daughter."

"A daughter! One of my sisters survived?"

"I have heard so," the old woman said.

"Where is she now? Do you know where she is living now?" Manco asked urgently.

"I know only that there was a son and a daughter. Nothing more."

"But who told you this, Señora?"

The old woman's face went blank. She did not answer.

"Do you recall who told you that a son and a daughter had survived?"

"You see that I am muy anciana. Whoever it was that told me must now be dead."

"But how did you recognize me?"

"I do not know. In your face, something."

"Would you recognize my sister?"

"I do not know. She was so young. I cannot now recall her face, Señor."

"Do you recall her name?"

"No. What is your own name?"

"I am Manco."

"Manco . . . I think I remember this name. But I am not certain. I would not have thought of it myself."

Manco did not know what to say. Suddenly to have this startling information revealed, and no sooner revealed—then obscured again.

"Please, Señora, this is of very great importance to me. Strain your memory. Is there anyone at all who might have even the slightest information about my family?"

The old woman thought for a moment. "I am sorry, Señor Manco. I can think of nobody now alive who would have this information."

"Then can you tell me anything? About my father, my family?"

After a long pause the old woman said: "Tupac was a good man, and well-respected . . ." I cannot say anymore. I am muy anciana, as you can see."

"Yes. I thank you with all my heart for what you have told me, Señora. Que le vaya bien—May all go well with you."

When the old woman left, Manco turned to his friend.

"You heard, Inti?"

"Yes."

"What should I do, my friend?"

"What can you do? Continue as before. Be patient. Believe in your music."

Manco accepted his friend's counsel. It was not easy. The turbulence occasioned by the old woman's recognition of him was too much with him. It was enough for him simply to push it out of mind. For it to flourish out of mind, into song, it would have to be much longer, or at least more securely, buried.

Manco even found himself welcoming visitors, accepting the questions of Cruces and Gringos in the Plaza de Armas. Any distraction served to keep him from tormenting himself with questions about his family, his sister. The result was not only that he thought less, but that he began to respond more agreeably to people. Formerly, Manco reserved his agreeable responses only for those who *heard* his music. For the others he maintained a stiff and reticent courtesy. That was the way it had been from as early as he could remember. Manco had no idea how he had been as a child in the city of Cuzco. He supposed different; innocent, unguarded, having legs to walk on, run. Probably he had been like Inti, who said that since his interior world was always the same, he himself remained a "child."

After playing in the Quechua Plaza from early morning until mid-day, the two musicians returned to their hut to have their lunch of potatoes and beans and fruit, or yacuchupe, a green soup made with potatoes, peppers, and various herbs. Then they rested. Or if there were visitors, they played music and talked a little.

The two young German "sponsors" returned to their hut and presented the musicians with a long neatly-printed list, which they had had translated into Spanish. This list contained all the information about the "tour" they wanted the musicians to make, and it included the money they would earn on each stop of the tour.

Their Cruce interpreter explained: "The entire tour will last only thirty days, compadres. Your hosts," he pointed to the two young men, "have seen to everything. You will fly in a plane from Cuzco to the city of Lima. There you will change to a very large airplane which will fly you directly to the great city of Frankfurt in Alemania. You will live in fine hotel rooms and eat the best food"—here the Cruce was interrupted by one of the Germans who said something in his language.

"Don Helmut reminds me to tell you that the cooks of his country will prepare for you the food to which you are accustomed, if that is your wish. All you need do, compadres, is play your instruments as you play in the Plaza de Armas. And when the tour is completed you will fly in one of our Peruano airplanes back here to Cuzco. Only you will not return as you left, hombres, because you will each have 2000 soles in your poncho."

"2000 soles!" Manco repeated.

"That is right, Cojito. 2000 soles *each*. How does that sound to you, friend Inti?"

"It is much money," Inti said.

"Claro! More than you and Cojito can make in a year. Between you!"

One of the Germans spoke.

"Don Federico suggests that you look closely at the schedule I have given to you."

"Yes," Inti said. "We will see you then afterwards in the plaza."

"You will have made a decision by then, don Inti?"

"Yes."

When the three left, Manco picked up the "schedule."

"I cannot read many of these words, Inti."

"Does it matter?"

"No. I do not wish to fly in an airplane to the country of the Alemanes."

"Nor do I," Inti said. "We will tell them so."

The Cruce interpreter was waiting for them at the fountain. The musicians slipped down from the llama and took their accustomed place.

"Well, my friends," the Cruce accosted them with nervous eyes, "what do you say?"

"We will not go, Señor." Inti returned the schedule to him. "Please thank the Señores for their generous offer."

The Cruce's eyes flashed with anger, but he said merely, "As you wish," biting off the words. Then he turned away.

Meanwhile people were greeting the musicians in Quechua, in Spanish.

Manco and Inti commenced to play. When the small bowl was filled with centavos, Manco transferred the coins to a bolsa, then replaced the bowl. The Indios who listened generally gave food: causa or carapulca or chuñu. Manco placed the food in the bolsa as well.

The bells in the Iglesias chimed loudly for each hour. And a band was performing at the western end of the plaza. And today two other Quechua musicians from the mountains above Cuzco played their music. They moved around the plaza, one playing the pan-pipes and the other the quena. They performed wayno and popular tunes from the cinema, as well as an occasional yaravi. Both were skillful musicians.

Manco and Inti scarcely noticed the competing sounds and movements that were always around them. Inti wrapped about his harp was never outside the music, and Manco more and more remained with his quena, allowing the outside sounds to pass through him.

Once, several months after the Indios had declined the Germans' offer, Manco said to Inti as they were riding up the hill to their hut: "For me it was much easier today. When we played I heard nothing but our music."

"That is good, Cojito."

"You have told me," Manco said, "that what you see within when you play is what you have always seen. What is it that you have always seen, Inti?"

They rode for a time before Inti responded.

"To a child the world appears filled with space, is not that so, Cojito?"

"Yes."

"At the same time the child's world is íntimo, since everything he sees he becomes: animal, plant, mountain . . . And all these things are glazed with the child's light, which is also, I believe, the light of all things. When I stroke the harp this fine space opens within me."

Manco tried to comprehend these words.

"And if we had gone in the airplane with the Alemanes to their country, would it have been different? Would you have seen this space there as well, Inti?"

"I do not know how it would be in the country of the Alemanes, my friend. I know only how it is in our own."

VII   EL CÓNDOR

One night Manco was awakened by a loud knocking on the door.

"Pase, pase," Manco called from his mat.

A Quechua boy holding a lighted splinter of cone wood entered.

"You are the son of Tupac the woodcutter?"

"I am."

"La vieja, the old woman who knew your people, said to tell you that your sister was taken to the village of Tacna after the great earthquake.

"The village of Tacna?"

"That is what she said."

"She said nothing else?"

"That is all she said, Señor."

When the boy left, Manco tried to sleep, but could not still his mind. When Inti awoke before dawn, Manco told him.

"The old woman—she remembered."

"Yes."

"Where is the village of Tacna, Inti?"

"It is to the east, on the other side of the sierra."

"It is a difficult journey?"

"It is a difficult journey, my friend."

"I must go."

"Yes. Take the llama, but be careful, he is old now, not so strong as formerly."

"I will be careful. I will leave tomorrow. Today I will ask Tambo to make me a map."

"Yes."

"My sister, Inti. I will see her after all these years."

Tambo was an old Quechua who worked with wool. Manco found him in his accustomed place, squatting against his mud brick hut in the hills above the Quechua Plaza. Tambo was knitting with brown and white alpaca wool.

"Muy buenos días, Tambo."

"Ah, Cojito. Buenos días. No music this morning, my friend?"

"Not this morning. I am preparing to go to the village of Tacna."

"Tacna, is it? You must then go soon. For the feria."

"What is this feria, Tambo?"

"Why it is the feria of Yawar. The ceremony of blood. It is well-known."

"I am going for another matter," Manco said. "I plan to leave tomorrow. Can you make me a map, Tambo?"

"Yes, my friend. Why not?"

Manco slipped down from the llama and slid next to the old man.

"You have brought paper?" Tambo asked, his needles dexterously looping the wool.

"I have." Manco took out a sheet of paper and a black crayon from his poncho. "That is fine wool, Tambo."

"Claro. The best alpaca. From the Altiplano. Do you go with Inti to the village of Tacna?"

"I go alone, viejo."

"Pues. It is better. I do not think the llama would be able to carry two. Not to Tacna."

"How long is it, Tambo?"

"You leave tomorrow before the sun, you will be three days going. On the fourth morning you will arrive in Tacna.

If you follow the map," the old man laughed, his needles working rhythmically at the wool. "That will be just in time for Yawar."

"And the rains?"

"Not for another thirty days. No sooner. But take your chullo. It is cold in the eastern sierra."

Manco nodded.

"Muy bien." The old man set down his needles. "I will make you a fine map."

The map in his poncho, Manco made his way back to the Quechua Plaza. As in the Plaza de Armas, the musicians sat beneath the statue, near the fountain. Except that here the Castellano on his rearing horse was badly chipped, and the fountain was without water.

Inti, playing wayno, was surrounded by compadres. When they saw Manco they welcomed him.

"Ah, friend Cojito, we thought we would not hear from you this morning."

Manco smiled as he slid next to Inti.

That afternoon and evening Manco played as usual in the Plaza de Armas. But he did not play with an empty mind.

Inti made no reference to his journey until later that night as they were returning from the plaza.

"You are ready then, my friend?"

"Yes," Manco said.

The following day while it was still dark, they embraced.

"Goodbye, Inti. I will return as soon as I learn."

"Goodbye, my friend."

"I will return soon. Cuzco is my home."

"Goodbye, Cojito."

By the time Manco reached the cone forest high above the city, the sun was rising and the garúa was thick about him. He knew he had done this many times before, on foot, following the slender, agile figure with the rope wrapped around his waist, carrying his sling and axe and machete. Into the garúa.

Manco stopped to lash himself tightly to the llama. The trail was already becoming steep. They had moved into the sierra.

He wondered about her, his sister, whether she too had gone with them to the cone forest. Or did she remain at home with his mother? Aunt Soledad had said there were two sisters. Manco recalled nothing about them. Could she, the surviving one, still be living in Tacna? With whom? Perhaps Manco's family had relatives in Tacna. Though Aunt Soledad had never mentioned the village of Tacna. Never that he remembered.

The rising sun's fire was gone. Now he felt the sun's heat on his head through the garúa-mist. The clouds looked like finely spun alpaca wool as they moved from south to north.

Tambo had told him of four difficult passes. The first would be coming up within three or four kilometers. Manco brushed his llama's head affectionately. Aloud he said:

"Llamita, my friend. My old friend, I wish I might be as you, without thought. Without fear. Silent in every kind of weather." Manco smiled. "You are more like Inti than you are like me. He too is silent in every weather. And at his harp he plays of silence. Yes, you are closer to Inti than to me. And you are the more fortunate for it."

He recalled the little llama talisman Aunt Soledad had given him. He had long ago lost it.

Lagartijas—small lizards—scuttled back and forth across his path. Manco thought he might have intruded upon a lizard pueblo. And now they were showing their disapproval. Even as he framed this thought he turned sharply around the sierra, startling a cóndor who flew off with a lizard in his beak.

"What is this, Condorito? You have stooped to eating lizards?" Manco made a clucking sound and shook his head.

The borrachos are lizards, their bodies jerking in the gutter. Swallowing, swallowing, waiting for the great bird. Swallowing their chicha, waiting. No, Inti's acceptance of his compadres' suffering could not be Manco's. What then? Would the little cripple brandish his quena at El Cóndor? Condorito eats cojitos as well as drunks. He eats Cruces too. And Castellanos. Yes, Castellanos too, since the great bird flying so close to the sun can appreciate the fine white meat. He does not eat—Manco smiled sardonically—statues of Castellanos on horseback. He has not the stomach for it.

The trail was narrowing, the footing becoming difficult. The llama was kicking up loose clay and stones with every step. The stones echoed hollowly as they fell into the canyon below. The first dangerous pass was up ahead. Tambo had said that the difficulty here was the wind, that Manco should keep close to the sierra wall. Manco did this, and the fierce wind swept the llama closer still, so that in spite of Manco's efforts the llama was dislodging stones from the wall with his flank. The pass itself was no more than two meters wide. After Manco got across he examined the llama's flank. It was bruised, though not bleeding.

"With legs I could have kept you away from the wall, llamita. Forgive me, my friend."

Glancing behind him, Manco saw that the cóndor, a male with the crest and white throat, was now perched on a peak on the other side of the pass. Manco shouted to him.

"O Cóndor, you peer into the mountain's throat. Do you see a cripple, Condorito? Perhaps you see a borracho. He is drunk from chicha, and now his jerking body makes him easy to see, even far down there in the gutter. In the mountain's throat. You have fine eyes, Condorito. The hook of your mouth is also fine. Only take care that you do not sink your hook into that Castellano on horseback. His skin is steel, O Cóndor."

The cóndor, his neck hunched close to his body, did not move.

"You wait like a monk of the church to suck up our dead," Manco said. "You see in us the death behind our living. You see this thing with your keen eyes. Yet that is all you see, Condorito."

The sun was high in the sky. The clouds were large, intricate, very white.

"Those are not clouds," Manco said. "Those are llamas. Thousands of llamas. See how gently they move." To himself he said: "I never recognized this before."

Manco rode faster now, wanting to cover as much ground as he could while there was light. The trail was winding up gradually. Above him the ridges were tipped with snow. One of the passes Tambo mentioned was through the snow. But that would be in the morning, before the sun was high enough to turn the snow into water.

When Manco saw the small black and white birds with the notched tails circling and diving beneath him in the canyon, he paused and removed the map. It was close to sunset. Tambo had told him of a rock overhang on a wider portion of the trail that was protected from the wind. The sheer side of the trail contained enough grass to fodder the llama. Now Manco would try to find this place before it was dark. It had already become colder, windier, the wind blowing hard from the northwest.

Ahead of him Manco saw his camping place. It was as Tambo said. Manco untied his body, untied also the bolsa containing food, and slipped off the llama.

"Go, my good friend, feed on the grass. And tomorrow early you will have water."

Manco slid against the wall beneath the overhang. It gave off to the east and the south. He took a few sips of water from his gourd, then ate some of the chuñu—dried potatoes he had wrapped in newspaper. In the distance he saw the cóndor hovering over a ridge, suddenly wheel and dive into the canyon.

"Eat, Condorito. Even I who can only crawl on my hip, eats. You who are wider than five cripples, who soar and dive as fast as sight, need much fuel. Eat then. Wheel and dive and kill, that you may eat."

Manco looked up at the clouds, pink and orange from the dying sun. He took out his quena and played.

The llama, attracted by the music, ambled towards him.

"You are a strange llama. You could not have eaten much good grass, and yet when you hear the quena you forget your food. Muy bien, I will play for you.

Manco played yaravi.

"That was for you, llamita. It was for the sierra and for the throat of the sierra. It was even for the white-throated bird with the casco on his head. Though I think he did not hear it. This music of joy in sadness Condorito will not hear. It is not this music that he hears when he dives into the mountain's throat."

Manco picked up a stone and threw it into the canyon, hearing the distant echo. He did it again. He gazed up at the clouds: "Llamitas. On their flanks, on their heads, on their backs . . ."

He picked up another stone and threw it into the canyon.

"If the clouds are llamas what are these stones that I throw into the mountain's throat? I do not know what they are—unless they are Indios. Are not these stones made up of sand, of earth, of the mountains alive beneath the earth? And who has fed this earth more than Indios have fed it?"

Manco picked up another stone, turning it over in his fingers.

"What do you think of this stone, llamita? This small round stone? How many Indios' lives are frozen in this stone, my friend?"

Manco examined the stone closely.

"How many Indio borrachos' lives are frozen in this stone?"

He dropped the stone down into the canyon.

"Do you hear the little sound, llamita? When the Condorito hears that sound he does not hear it. Though it may be the sound of twenty Indios, El Cóndor does not hear it. But wait, my friend, there is yet another sound that is also of Indios, it comes from the mountains alive beneath the earth. It is this sound I have heard most clearly, llamita. I do not understand it. But when the earth shakes again a piece of me will be in it, stone or root or mountain."

And his sister? Did his sister escape whole from the shaking?
He should have asked the old woman. She could not have known.

Manco slept.

Manco was up and mounted before dawn. Today they
would see snow. The first turn up-mountain took him into
the wind—it whipped his head around, and would have
toppled him into the canyon had he not been tightly lashed
to the llama. The first faint glimmers of the sun were on the
horizon. According to Tambo, there would be a stream
flowing northwest within the next kilometer.

Manco saw the stream. When he got to it he drank,
then filled his gourd. He waited for the llama who was very
thirsty. The birds were awake, skimming the stream, calling to each other, greeting the sun.

"You are drinking all of the insects, llamita. What will
the birds do?"

Manco recalled the campesino who had taken him from the
Altiplano to the village of Oroya. He recalled how greedily he
himself had drunk his maté, burning his palate. He had drunk his
maté as a llama drinks water from a stream.

The sun had risen. The morning was cloudless. One of
the stars from the night had not yet faded. Manco continued up-mountain. After some 200 meters the gradual
inclination became steeper. The hard wind whistled, blowing sand and loose stones against the llama's hooves. Soon
Manco had to shield his face with his pañuelo. He rode
slowly, close to the sierra wall. He knew by the bite of the
wind that they were close to snow. And then, turning
sharply east, he was into it: patches of snow underfoot,
framing the cliff face, much more snow above him. The
snow was hard. It would have to be hard above him for him
to cross the pass which would be coming up soon. Manco
heard hooves and the sound of wheels: someone was coming down-mountain.

A carreta—a cart loaded with supplies and drawn by
two oxen. Behind it a man on mule-back. They saw Manco

and waited for him at a wider portion of the trail. The man on the cart was Indio, the other Cruce.

"Dónde va?" the Cruce shouted.

"To the village of Tacna."

"We have just come. It is a village of pigs, this Tacna. There is nothing to do there, I assure you."

"Is there not the feria?"

"Ah, Yawar. I have seen it before."

"Is the snow above firm?" Manco asked.

"Claro. You are not much more than a kilometer from the pass. You will cross without a problem. We did—but then these brutos," motioning to the oxen, "never go down. How is it below?"

"Much wind. But the footing is not bad."

"Muy bien, pues. Hasta la próxima—until the next time, friend. I am anxious to get to the city of Cuzco."

"Adios," Manco said, passing them.

The Indio in the cart had said nothing.

The footing near the pass was firm, as the Cruce had said. It was difficult to see with the wind swirling the snow, but Manco steered the llama over the ridge the oxen had made coming down. Soon the trail would wind down-mountain for two kilometers, and then settle into an even grade, where after three or four kilometers more Manco would find the path that led to a stream, which would be their camping place.

Riding down-mountain Manco's body was forced against the ropes that lashed him to the llama. His body was sore and bruised from the pressure of the ropes, but that did not matter. He was more than halfway to the village of Tacna. Again he wondered whether his sister was still living in this village, and also who had taken her there to begin with. He was almost certain that neither his aunt nor his uncle had ever mentioned Tacna, which meant that they had not known his sister survived.

He looked at the sky. The sun was declining. In the sun's shadow Manco on his llama appeared as a single figure. Except that in truth the llama was a cloud, and Manco was a stone.

Manco's mind was a stone. It had always been so and was yet, in spite of Inti. In spite of yaravi. Manco recalled his old friend, the chaki, saying that the Indios in the hills felt that he possessed "power." He was broken, he survived, he made music on a pipe, so he possessed power. His mind was a stone.

"My mind is a stone, llamita. And Inti's mind is a stream of fresh-running water. Inti's mind is nourished by rain, snow, sun, and the river. The river is nourished by the sea. If a stone sinks to the bottom of Inti's stream it remains there, until perhaps it too becomes, gradually becomes, water."

The llama did not reply.

"Pues, you already know all this. Yet it is new to me. Ah, there are the small birds with the pointed wings and notched tails. The great fliers. We must now look for the stream on Tambo's map."

A narrow dirt path cut crosswise down–mountain. It curved steeply at first, but then leveled . . . And there was Tambo's stream.

Unharnessed, Manco sat next to the stream, resting, watching the llama drink. Then he lay back and looked up at the clouds. He felt very tired. He removed some cone twigs from his bolsa, gathered rocks and dry grass, and prepared a fire. He put a small pot of water on the fire and dropped some coca leaves into it. Then he turned towards the stream again. The small birds with the notched tails were diving with high-pitched trills, skimming the water for insects. Manco heard the twigs crackling on the fire, he smelled the wood scent, he closed his eyes. When he opened them he saw a dragonfly darting and skating on the stream very close to him. The delicate stick of its body was the color of the horizon, sky becoming grass beneath the sun. Manco removed his quena and, watching the dragonfly, accompanied its sudden silent zigzags on the water . . .

"Very pretty, this music of yours, dragonfly. This music that is your feeding. But I am not sure I understand it. Let me try again."

This time Manco played wayno, leaving room between measure and phrase for the movements of the dragonfly, for the feeding dance of the dragonfly on the lighted water . . .

"That was better. But if I give space in the wayno to your feeding, dragonfly, should I not give space also to the diving of the small birds, and to the cone wood on the fire, and to the play of wind in the canyon? That would be a fine music, would it not? It would be silence." Manco smiled. "I will have to ask Inti about this silent music."

As Manco turned to the maté on the fire, he glimpsed the cóndor diving into the canyon out of sight.

The village of Tacna lay before him. It appeared smaller even than Oroya, which perhaps would make it easier for him to find out about his sister. It was early morning. Manco thought he would begin in the Indio quarter.

He approached a very old woman, an herb-seller.

"With permission, Señora, I am looking for a woman who is the daughter of Tupac the woodcutter, from the city of Cuzco."

The old woman said she knew nothing of this person, but directed him to another vieja across the road. This second woman also knew nothing. She suggested that Manco consult the padre in the Iglesia. Manco could see the Iglesia from where he was. It was of course the highest structure in the village. When he got to it he was told that a service was in progress. He waited in the courtyard, hearing the somber chords of the organ and a muted voice which belonged, he supposed, to the padre.

After the Indios and the Cruces, each group walking separately, made their way down the steps, Manco saw the padre, a small old man in a long black robe, slowly emerge from the Iglesia.

"Señor Padre, may I ask you something?" Manco shouted in Spanish.

The padre, looking around him, saw only an Indio on a llama.

Manco addressed him again, and this time the old man acknowledged him. He came slowly down the steps.

"With permission, Padre, I cannot dismount." Manco

pointed to his stumps. "I would like to ask you a question . . ."

The padre said that he did in fact recall a number of refugees from the great earthquake being brought to Tacna. As far as he knew most of them had left or died.

"But I cannot remember the matter at all clearly," the padre continued. "It was many years ago."

Manco nodded.

"There is one other possibility. One of my parishioners had been closely involved in the feeding and caring for the refugees. He will be here tomorrow for the feria. I will ask him about this woman. Her name is?"

"I do not know her name, Padre. She is the daughter of Tupac the woodcutter. She was a child of perhaps six or seven years when she was brought here."

"Tupac the woodcutter. I will remember." The padre turned and walked stiffly up the steps.

Manco watched him. He would ask others, and if he learned nothing he would wait until this friend of the padre arrived from Cuzco.

Manco rode back into the Indio quarter, where he inquired of several more people, without results. He made his way to the plaza in the center of the village. There elaborate arrangements were being made for the feria. A route from the plaza's entrance to a street perhaps 100 meters away had been sectioned off with painted ropes. Colorfully decorated stalls were being set up on either side of this route. Manco entered the plaza and rode up to the fountain, where he washed himself in the water. The llama drank and cropped the grass and low hedges near the fountain.

Manco took out his quena and played. In a matter of minutes he was surrounded by listeners. He played wayno, moving fluidly from one embellishment to another, ending with the variation he had discovered while sitting by the stream and observing the dragonfly. When he put down his quena an Indio with a shaved head inquired whether he had come for the feria.

"I have come for another reason," Manco said.

"Pues. You are fortunate. The feria of Yawar is very beautiful."

"Yes?"

"Claro. For us Indios it is truly very beautiful. As you will see, my friend."

That night Manco slept in the campo at the edge of the village. When he returned to the plaza in the morning, the stalls were set up, and two great effigies, one on the plaza side, the other on the street side at the opposite end of the route, had been suspended from ropes. The effigy near the plaza represented a bearded man in white armor brandishing a sword. The other was the image of a Quechua dressed in the ancient costume.

Though it was just past dawn, the plaza was already filling with people who were talking and laughing with much spirit. Entire families of Indios were camped on the grass with their children and mules or llamas. And many more families were moving into the area. Manco bought a bowl of yacu-chupe from one of the stalls and settled himself on the grass in a corner of the plaza. A man sitting next to him with his family was swigging chicha. He passed the small bottle to Manco.

"No, friend. I don't drink this," Manco said, handing the bottle back to him.

The Indio was offended. "Drink, hombre! Only the Cruces remain dry today. Yawar," he poked his chest with his fingers, "is for us! It is our day today!" He pushed the bottle at Manco.

Manco took a swallow and returned the bottle to the man.

"Muy bien," the Indio grinned. "Chichita!" He took another swallow and passed the bottle to his wife. She drank also.

The man, who was already drunk, picked up his machete from the grass, removed a small file from his poncho, and rubbed the blade of the machete to sharpen it. Holding his arm out in front of him he made a small incision above his wrist. He grinned at Manco. Then he took the arm of his son, a boy of seven or eight years, and bloodied his wrist. He allowed the blood from his son's arm and his own to drip onto the grass, then he pressed the arms together, blood to blood, keeping them together for several seconds. He patted his son's head and turned to Manco.

"Yawar!" he pronounced hoarsely, his eyes filled with tears. "It is to exalt our blood."

Manco looked at him without speaking, then removed his quena and began to play softly . . .

"Cojo," the drunk Indio said, brushing Manco's shoulder affectionately with his hand.

Manco played softly with his eyes open. The sun was lifting and the sky was clear. The purple snow-tipped mountains surrounded the plaza on every side. Manco's llama had found another llama. They stood side by side quietly, occasionally nuzzling the hedges. The mingled smells of food, chicha, animals and people were very strong. Of the hundreds of people in the area, Manco did not spot more than five or six Cruces. Judging from their outfits, the Quechuas were mostly from Tacna and the hills nearby. Manco wondered about the padre's friend from the city of Cuzco, whether he had yet arrived. If Manco did not see the priest at the feria he would go to the Iglesia in the morning.

Several children had now pushed close to Manco to listen to the lilting wayno, and were dancing and jumping high-spiritedly—when the loud, mournful drone of a horn sounded above him. Manco put down his quena. The horn sounded again: several extended mournful notes vibrating above the plaza. It was a thrilling sound, and the children gazed at each other with wonder in their eyes.

"Wajra-pukara," one boy said aloud. "It is to call our people to the Yawar."

The horn sounded still another time.

The wajra-pukara was blown periodically from mid-morning until sunset, as the plaza and surrounding areas continued to fill with people. Only the roped-off area, the route between the two great effigies, was kept free.

By the time the sun commenced to sink, the children

who had been listening to Manco's music were becoming restless. They fought with each other playfully and darted through and around the legs of people nearby. Some of the children paired off: one on his hands and knees, the other mounted on his back, and played "Yawarita," the child on the ground attempting to topple the rider.

The sun had just disappeared behind the sierra when the wajra-pukara sounded again, louder and longer—and suddenly there was activity in the roped-off area. In order to see Manco swung onto the llama and allowed himself to be swept along in the crowd that was pushing towards the ropes. The activity had begun at the other end of the route, but appeared to be moving towards the plaza. Then Manco—astonished—saw: a male cóndor was mounted on a great white bull. The bull's back had been pierced and the cóndor's talons attached to the back with sinew. Colored tassels had been sewn into the bull's ears. Indios on horseback stationed all along the route poked at the bull with long poles, driving him forward between the ropes. The enraged bull pulled and jerked, twisting its body, desperately trying to release himself from the furious bird; the cóndor, beating its huge wings, hissing, hacking with its beak at the bull's head and neck.

Each time the bull was driven by them, the Indios, crowding against the ropes, cursed it in Spanish and Quechua:

"Maldito . . . "
"Toro cabrón . . . "
"Mancho . . . "
(While praising the cóndor):
"Pureza . . . "
"Querida alma . . . "
"Espíritu . . . "

It continued in this way for some time, up and down the roped area, until the bull was trailing blood and both creatures were exhausted. Then, in the center of the route, the bull was halted, and with a few strokes of the machete the cóndor was released and thrown into the air, where it took wing, hovered for a moment, and lifted away with bleeding chunks of the bull's skin still sewn to its talons. The people cheered wildly above the loud wild drone of the wajra-pukara.

The white bull, numbed and bleeding, was coaxed into a wooden cage and taken away.

Afterwards, as Manco was riding through the plaza, he overheard the people talking. The feria of Yawar apparently represented the Indios' conquest of their Castellano oppressors. The bull, an animal first brought by the conquistadores, was the invader, and the native cóndor represented the soaring Indio spirit. Strange. On the journey from Cuzco Manco had addressed the cóndor as death. Here he represented the spirit of life. "Death," "life," they were after all only words.

Manco had not seen the padre at the feria, so now he was making his way to the Iglesia.

"Hola, Cojo."

Someone was calling him. It was the man from the day before, with the shaved head.

"Cojo, you saw the feria of Yawar?"

"Yes."

"It was very beautiful, was it not? I have seen it every year for the the last five years."

"Every year?"

"Sí, hombre! Yawar is held at the end of every year. To give us strength for the year to come."

"Ah."

"That is so. The Cruces—they too have a feria. But at the beginning of the year. Do you know of it?"

"No," Manco said.

"Pues. It is called 'Cóndor-Rachi.' The Cruces hang a condorito from a native tree and beat it with clubs. When it is dead the head Cruce bites the tongue out. Then it is flung into the crowd who tear it apart. The brutos! For them it means the death of our spirit. But they do not know us, hombre. They do not know the meaning of spirit."

Manco listened without speaking.

"Well, I go now," the man said. "Que le vaya bien.
May it go well with you, Cojo."

"Igualmente. To you too, Señor."

When Manco got to the Iglesia he saw that it was dark
within. He did not know whether the padre had returned
and gone to sleep, or had not yet returned. He decided to
wait. He slid off the llama and sat on the steps. After a time
he played his quena softly. He played yaravi, thinking of
the ritual he had just witnessed. His feelings about it were
uncertain. Then he thought about his sister. What if the
padre's friend could supply no information? Pues, in that
case Manco would return to Cuzco empty. Yet Manco felt
somehow that this friend of the padre would have something for him. Manco played yaravi and gazed at the black
sky filled with stars. He knew them well, the group called
the "Scythe," the "Fish" near the eastern horizon, the
cluster that resembled a great bird with outstretched wings,
and of course the clearly etched "Humpback," which was
an extension of the great bird. They were familiar old pres-
ences which had ceased to terrify. Manco observed them as
he did the lights in and around the Plaza de Armas in
Cuzco: beautiful, cold, separate from him . . .

The sound of a carro stopping close to the Iglesia.
Talking, laughing. The padre and two Castellanos emerg-
ing from the carro, walking towards the steps.

"Con permiso, Señor Padre."

The startled old priest turned in the opposite direction.

Manco called again as he swung himself onto the
llama. This time the padre saw him. Manco rode over to
them.

"The matter about your sister, is it? This gentleman
will answer your inquiry." The padre gestured to one of the
white-haired Castellanos.

"Yes, then, what was her name? This sister of yours?"
the Castellano wished to know.

"I do not know her given name, Señor. She was the
daughter of Tupac the woodcutter. She was, I think, a child
of six or seven years at the time—"

"Oh yes. Of course. She lived here for some time," the
Castellano said. "With a distant relative, an old woman

who died some years ago. In fact she was here again not too long ago. With her child. Are you Raymi's brother, Cojo?"

"What?"

"Are you Raymi's brother? She thought that her entire family had been taken—"

"Raymi?" Manco repeated.

"Yes. That is her name. Raymi."

"Her son's name?" Manco demanded.

The Castellano appeared surprised at Manco's insistence. "I do not recall."

"Was it Yaravi?"

The Castellano looked at the cripple for a moment before answering.

"Yes, Yaravi, that was the name."

. . . Manco managed to find his way back to the plaza, where he spent the night without sleep. The following morning before the sun he rode up into the hills in the direction of Cuzco. But then he turned back, rode into the Indio quarter of Tacna, stopped in a tienda and bought a bottle of chicha which he swallowed as fast as he could stomach it. Then, leaning against the fractured wall of the tienda, he fell into a dazed sleep.

When he awoke with his mind working, he bought more chicha and repeated the process.

After several days of this Manco found himself without soles, and so was obliged to play his quena. He did not play in a particular place, but wherever he happened to find himself: in the Indio quarter; below, near the plaza; en route. Wherever he played, he drank and slept, as he was usually too unsteady to hoist himself onto his animal. He wanted only to deaden his mind. Chicha did it for him. Soles were necessary to purchase chicha. Where or how he accumulated the few soles he needed each day did not matter.

The sun which had always corresponded to the force within him, was now as indifferent as night. That the weather was neither excessively cold nor wet, meant he could sleep wherever he lay. That was all he observed or wished to observe.

Not even the chicha was always successful in numbing the press of his mind, which mercilessly spat back at him the distorted images of his great pecado. Sin—pecado— was a concept Manco had never before considered. Before it never applied to his life. Now it enveloped him, having sprung dreadful and echoing from the mouth of the Castellano on the steps of the Iglesia. His pecado enveloped him, transforming every thought or feeling into some semblance of itself. When the chicha failed to work Manco was slung abruptly back into the groin of this pecado. The pain here was so great that he would push his head against whichever earth he lay upon and press his fists against his ears . . . Then he would swallow more chicha.

The "time" within his mind, when not muted, remained stuck to that dread place in the hills of Puno. And yet time had not stopped, the seasons continued pushing in, then out, of each other. One night after the coming of the rains, an Indio in a cart nearly ran over the drunk and sopping cripple. He gathered Manco up and transported him to shelter, a lean-to that harbored the neighboring stock animals. Here Manco remained with his llama, sleeping on the earthen floor, paying the owner a few centavos a night.

The bad weather meant too that Manco earned less from his music. Yet he earned enough to pay for his chicha. The music itself had become slack and redundant, and the coins dropped into the cripple's chullo were dropped out of pity. Manco was of course no longer young and the conditions of his life were rapidly weakening him. It took all his strength to hoist himself onto the llama, and usually he fell once or twice in the attempt. On some days he did not even try to mount the animal, but sat against the lean-to with his flute in his lap and—when he saw someone approach—with his chullo outstretched.

As to sleep, Manco swallowed himself into a stupor which was neither sleep nor waking. But then his body would recoil and he would sleep for as long as two days at a time. The first time this occurred, the lean-to landlord thought he was dead and engaged two beggars to dispose of the carcass. But as they were wrapping the body in newspaper, one of the beggars heard breathing. They informed the landlord. Hours later the cripple found himself awake . . .

One evening during the season of rain, Manco found himself awake, his chullo empty of centavos, and the weather apparently clear. He struggled to his llama and tried to hoist himself aboard, but did not have nearly the strength. He called to an Indio passing by who lifted him onto the animal. Manco had no idea where he wanted to go, but the llama headed downhill, towards the plaza. The weather was unnaturally clear for the season. The sky, Manco saw without seeing, as he looked ahead of him, was moonless, alive with stars. The llama entered the plaza and ambled to the fountain. There he stopped. Manco, who had been largely insensible during the ride, suddenly recognized his surroundings and tumbled off the animal. Painfully he slid over to his accustomed place beneath the statue, then stuck his hand in his poncho for the quena—it was not there. He moved his hands along his body, but the quena was gone. It had somehow gotten lost. Manco pulled off his chullo and turned it inside out on his lap. There were no coins in it. He stopped, again lapsing into insensibility. But then he recovered and, with a great effort, regained a certain concentration. Methodically now, he searched every fold in his poncho, he searched his trousers, he looked again in his chullo. The quena was gone. It was gone and he did not have a single centavo. His head was whirling. He struggled over to the basin and thrust his face into the cold water, fed for so many weeks by the rain. When he withdrew his head it did not feel better. He did it again, this time remaining under water for several seconds, feeling already a certain giving way. He withdrew his head again, no longer dazed, but compelled by the sudden vision of the blankness he had felt beneath the water. Death was beneath the water. Not the mimic death of chicha. Death. Manco was about to fall headlong into the basin for a final time, when someone shined light in his face . . . It was the reflection of the black sky's light in his face. The stars. Manco gazed into the water at the stars. He gazed at the stars with a sudden and curious calmness. It had been so long since he had seen them. And yet they were there as always. Brighter. Swaying a little in the clear, cold water. Directly above him was the great bird, the cóndor, with its wings outspread. And two of the stars that made up one of the wings were also portion of the "Humpback." Bird and humpback were connected. They were a single thing.

Manco slept by the fountain. All the next day he remained in the plaza begging centavos. Not for chicha—for food, potatoes, chuñu, and coca leaves for maté. Manco had decided to return to the city of Cuzco the following dawn.

Several of the Indios who dropped coins into his chullo seemed surprised at his condition.

"What's this?" one said. "You have enough in your chullo for two day's chicha. What are you saving for?"

Manco merely smiled.

The stars had just begun to fade when Manco, tightly lashed to the llama, moved up out of Tacna into the hills which led to the sierra. He no longer had the map which had guided him to Tacna many months before. He did not need it.

By the time Manco reached the snow-tipped ridges, it had begun to rain, so that he would have to wait until the following dawn's frost froze the water before crossing. He waited, camped in the thin-aired cold beneath the black, clouded sky. The stars: the great bird, the humpback, were gone. They were not gone. Manco, wrapped in his poncho, lying on the wet cold ground, knew they had never gone. He thought of Inti. It had been so long since he had thought of his friend and teacher. Now he thought of him with all the old affection.

Dawn came. It was clear and cold and the snow had hardened. As Manco made his way high into the sierra he came across an Apachita—a mound of stones adorned with smaller stones, twigs of cone wood, articles of clothing.

Manco had not seen this Apachita on his journey to Tacna. He undid the rope that lashed him to the llama, removed some coca leaves from his poncho, and added them to the shrine. Instinctively he felt inside his poncho for his quena—but then he remembered. It would have been good to make an offering of his music to the Apachita. Instead Manco bowed his head, touching it to the cold earth.

Once in Cuzco, Manco went directly to the hut. Inti was gone, playing in the Quechua Plaza. Within, the hut was the same. Manco's mat was in its old place beneath the wooden opening that served as a window. The mat was covered with the brown rebozo his pupil, Ricardo, the Gringo, had given to him as a gift. Manco slid over to the mat and lay down. He felt in his bones a great fatigue. Yet he did not sleep, but lay with his eyes open, his mind without thought. When he moved his body a little he felt something beneath him. He put his hand under the mat and removed a quena. He knew it was a quena immediately he touched it. He looked at it: it was not wood, but bone, the bone of an animal. It was the color of bone and exquisitely wrought. Manco put it to his lips . . . the tone he produced was even and fine. He was playing yaravi softly, tentatively, when Inti returned, entering quietly. Manco put down the quena.

"Play," Inti said, smiling. "It has been a while since I heard you play."

Manco played softly, carefully, without thought, listening to his notes with a mild surprise and a certain admiration, as if they were produced by another, who was yet himself.

"Yes," Inti said.

The two friends embraced.

"Where did it come from? This quena?"

"An old friend of yours, Cojito. A campesino Indio who transported wood on a llama. He said he had heard you were in the city of Cuzco and he wished to give you a recuerdo."

Manco of course remembered the campesino who had

taken him to Oroya, and then to Puno. He remembered the campesino's laugh.

"But where is he?"

"He is gone," Inti said. "He is long gone."

Manco looked again at the quena, fingering it, examining it tenderly. "It is bone," he said.

"It is bone from the wing of the great bird," Inti said. "El Condorito."

VIII YARAVI

$\mathbf{M}$anco rejoined Inti in the life he had left. The compadres in the Quechua Plaza were happy to see him and asked few questions about his long absence. In the afternoons the musicians rode downhill to the Plaza de Armas, which was just as it had been. And sometimes Manco rode up into the hills to play for the children. Wherever he was he played with pleasure. Never since that time many years before, when he had found the wooden quena in the rubbish pile in the village of Oroya, did Manco play with such pleasure. The spirit of the great bird doubtless remained in his instrument, and at certain moments which nearly always came unexpectedly, Manco's music merged with the bird in praise of it. The wayno praised it soaring aloft with the sun. The yaravi lamented its silent passing beyond the line of the horizon, the flame of its spent passion trailing behind it. It was in such or similar words that the campesino had explained it to him when they were passing above Lago Titicaca on the way to the city of Puno. It was, the campesino said, a legend of their people. Manco, who had forgotten it those many years, remembered it soon after he received the quena.

Slowly, over a period of weeks, Manco related to Inti

what had transpired in the village of Tacna. He told his
friend of the horrible revelation; of his subsequent constant
drunkenness; of the loss of his quena; of his near suicide
but for the light. He told of the cóndor and the humpback;
and of the ceremony of the bull and the bird, and of the
other ceremony called Cóndor-Rachi, in which the Cruces
murdered the bird.

Inti listened attentively, silently. When Manco, com-
pleting his narration, expressed wonder at how many
aspects of his life had become joined, Inti smiled.

It was only after Manco had been back for nearly two
years, that Inti made a suggestion.

"You have a sister, my friend. And you have a son.
Have you never thought of visiting them in the city of
Puno?"

Manco smiled faintly. "As usual you have somehow
divined my thoughts. I have been thinking increasingly of
my son. Of my sister. I would like to see them."

Inti nodded.

"The rains will begin in another month. I suppose I
should leave soon. But I am concerned about the llama. I do
not think he can easily make such a journey."

"You are right, Cojito. It is too long and difficult for
him now. But there are now carretas—carts being driven
between here and Puno. Carts of textiles and supplies.
They leave weekly. For ten soles they will take you."

"Yes, I have seen these carretas."

Four days afterwards Manco along with an old Cruce
was sitting in the wooden cart, squeezed between Cuzco
blankets and large wooden boxes of hardware. Three of
these narrow but sturdy carts, each drawn by two oxen, all
belonging to a wealthy Cruce supplier in the city of Lima,
traveled in tandem over the sierra.

At night the carretas encamped together, the drivers
promptly getting drunk on chicha, but recovering their
clarity abruptly at dawn. The entire journey turned out less
arduous than Manco had expected.

Puno itself looked the same, yet remote. Manco had
long ago separated his mind from his old city. Now he was

back. Instead of going immediately to the hut on the hill where the chaki had lived—where Raymi now lived with their son—he went first to see his friend Tana the quena-maker. He got a ride on a mule, and as the mule turned into the familiar calle, Manco saw his friend and Tampu, his apprentice, sitting in the old place, carving quenas.

"Ho!" Tana exclaimed, surprised. He got up to embrace his friend, as did Tampu, smiling.

"Cojito," Tana said.

"How are you, my friend?"

"I am as always. It has been a long time."

"Yes."

"You are well?" Tana asked.

"I am well, my friend."

"I am happy. Let us play then."

Manco slid to the wall next to his friends, and they played the wayno.

Afterwards, Tana asked to see Manco's quena. He examined it admiringly. "It is wrought from the bone in the cóndor's wing, is it not, Cojito?"

"Yes."

Tana passed the instrument to Tampu.

"Once before I saw and heard such a quena," Tana said. "An old Quechua from the village of Tacna beyond the eastern sierra. A master musician. He sometimes performed in the city of Cuzco, as you do, my friend. This was many years ago."

"Ah."

"Yes. And how is Master Inti?"

"Inti is as always," Manco said. "Older, as we all are. And yet not a day older."

Tana smiled.

"And Ricardo, the Gringo?" Manco asked.

"Ricardo has returned to his country," Tana said. "To make quenas out of wood. And to play the quena's music for his people."

"Ah. Are there not Indios in his country as well?" Manco asked.

"I believe there are, my friend."

Tampu handed the quena back to Manco. "It is a very fine instrument, Señor Cojo."

"It is. And you are doing well on your own quena, Tampu. The tone you make now is very clear."

"I thank you very much."

"Tell me, Tampu, is the woman Raymi living still in the chaki's hut?"

"I believe she is, Señor Cojo. I see her only on rare occasions in the mercado. But I see the son."

"I wish to visit with her. Can you give me a ride there, Tampu?"

Tampu mounted his mule and lifted Manco on behind him. As they made their way over the forgotten, yet utterly familiar, route to the chaki's hut, Manco struggled to keep his mind still. The terraced strips on which the chaki had planted potatoes and maize were overgrown. When they got to the hut Tampu asked whether he should wait.

"No, my friend. That is not necessary."

Manco waited until Tampu had ridden out of sight. Then he slid to the door and knocked. There was no reply. He moved towards the side of the house, beneath the shade of the roof. Several small neatly-tended strips of vegetables had been planted on this, the eastern, side of the hut. He sat there beside the garden, looking out over the hills of the city. Waiting. After a time he took out his quena and commenced to play. As he was playing he saw her. Raymi. She had walked slowly up the hill with a basket of supplies on her head. When she saw him she stopped, the expression in her eyes not so much surprise as uncertainty. She was uncertain about Manco's response to her. Manco continued to play, neither yaravi nor wayno, but another tune of the mountains. He played softly, his eyes partially open, looking at her. She scarcely resembled the woman he had known. She was old. And about her eyes, which Manco had remembered as filled with the light of passion—about her eyes was the grief of their loving. He put down the quena.

"Raymi." The familiar name felt strange on his lips.

"You have come."

"Yes."

Raymi set her basket on the ground and sat next to him. She moved with the deliberate movements of an old woman. For a time neither of them spoke.

"When did you know?" Manco asked softly.

"I felt it, or something, from the start," she said. "It was our bond I felt. But after we . . . loved, it was stronger. And it was somehow touched with—with pena. I asked questions about your past, and then I knew."

Manco did not respond.

"And the boy?" he asked finally.

"He is in school now. He is a fine boy. Strong and healthy."

"What does he know of his father?"

"Nothing. He knows nothing."

"But why did you call him Yaravi?" And why did you come back here, to the chaki's hut?"

"I did not come here right away. I returned to Tacna. And then we lived for a time in the city of Cuzco. When I decided to come to Puno, it was because I no longer felt shame. Our feelings for each other were true feelings. Our son is strong. Yaravi is the music of our struggle, our people's struggle, to remain strong. Nobody felt this music as you did, my brother."

Manco listened to these words. He himself could not say anything. But then, remembering, he said: "Why did you disappear as you did? From the very beginning you appeared, then disappeared, without a word. Then appeared again. It was the behavior"—he heard his voice going cruel—"of a courtesan."

Raymi turned her face to him. Her eyes had welled with water. She said: "I was frightened of the feeling that was growing in me. I was driven towards you, but I was also driven away by the closeness I felt to you. It seemed too close too suddenly."

"I am sorry," Manco said softly. "I should not have spoken so."

They remained silent, gazing out over the hills of the

city. The sun had already begun its decline. The sky was
cloudless, remote.

"You have suffered much, my brother."

Manco continued to gaze at the hills and at the mountains high behind them where they merged with the sky.

"Suffering, Raymi? What else is there?"

As he spoke these words he thought of Inti, of the
music.

"There is this," he said, holding up his quena. "It has
often been hard for me to remember that there is still the
music."

"I have never heard it played as you play it, Manco."

Manco turned to her. "What then will we tell the boy?"

"I have given thought to this," Raymi said. "I feel it is
best that we say you are his uncle. He will notice the
resemblance."

"Yes. Why is it we did not notice this resemblance?"

"I do not think it was then as it is now, Manco. We
have grown together by being apart."

"But the boy? You say he is healthy?"

"Yes, he is strong and healthy. It will not be long
before he becomes a man. He is already twelve years old."

"Ah."

"But now he is a boy, and he does what boys do. He is
very active." After a pause Raymi added, "Perhaps he is
also a little bit indulged. I was very protective of him in the
beginning."

"Yaravi," Manco tested his son's name on his lips.

"Yes. He will return from the school in a short time
now."

"How do you keep him?" Manco wondered. "And
yourself, and the hut?"

"I sew. I also weave with the hand loom, as our mother
once did."

"Our mother? I remember nothing of her hand loom,"
Manco said.

"I do not myself remember, but Santa, our mother's
aunt, with whom I lived in Tacna—Santa told me this."

"What else did she tell you, Raymi?"

"She spoke of our father, and of his particular love for his son. She said that you were a very unusual child. Aunt Santa said many of our people thought you were sagrado— touched by the saints."

Manco laughed at this.

"Once before, many years ago, I said to you that the Quechuas in the hills here in Puno spoke of your magic. You laughed then just as you laugh now."

Manco shrugged. "I am a cripple who plays a flute. If people choose to call this sagrado, or magical, they are welcome to it. But what else? Did she say anything else?"

"She said that the Quechuas in the hills of Cuzco said that but for me our entire family perished. And yet you too were rescued. It was with our father's sister that you lived on the Altiplano. Is that not so?"

"Yes."

"And she told you nothing?"

"She was not a woman who used words," Manco said. "And I asked nothing."

"She is dead now?"

"Yes, dead. I saw one of the cousins, Pepito, since Aunt Soledad died. He visited me in the city of Cuzco. He too is a musician." Manco recalled Pepito's innocent expression. "I should like to see him again."

"How then do you live now?" Raymi asked.

"I live with a dear friend. And teacher," Manco added. "We play music."

"Yaravi?"

"Yes. And wayno. And other music as well."

Manco heard loud talking from below.

"That is Yari," Raymi said.

The boy ran up the hill. When he saw his mother he stopped. "What are you doing here? And who is that with you?"

He came up to them and looked squarely at Manco. Manco recalled Raymi appearing in the same manner, walking boldly up to him that first time years ago. The boy seemed as his mother did then. His dark eyes lit with the same fire.

"This is your uncle Manco, my son. He has come from the city of Cuzco."

"My uncle? Is he the uncle you've told me about, Mamita? The músico?"

"Yes."

"But what happened to your legs, Uncle?"

"I lost them in the terremoto. The great earthquake in the hills of Cuzco."

"Is that your flute?"

"Yes."

"Play a tune. I should like to hear you play."

Manco took up his quena and played wayno, looking at the boy as he played. His son was handsome and seemingly healthy, but restless. His eyes darted. He tapped his foot . . .

"What kind of flute is it? What is it made of?"

"It is made of bone. The bone from the wing of the cóndor."

"Yes? Can I see it?"

Manco handed the boy his quena. He fingered it, put it to his mouth, blew into it a few times, and handed it back.

"Well! And why have you come to Puno, Uncle?"

"Puno was once my home. I have not been here in several years."

"Muy bien." He turned to his mother. "I should like to eat my dinner, Mamá."

"Yes. You will eat with us, Manco?"

"Yes."

Manco saw that the interior of the hut had been changed. There was now a table and chairs, and two cots were substituted for the bast mats that he remembered. There was even a small standing metal box filled with ice, in order to maintain the freshness of food.

Manco felt uneasy with his son. The fact that this straight-limbed, handsome, restless young man was his own creation—and his sister's—was inconceivable to him. Yet beneath his unease, Manco recognized the bond, the connection of blood, if not of spirit. Perhaps this deeper bond of the spirit would come afterwards.

For his "uncle," the boy appeared to feel nothing beyond a persistent, though natural enough, curiosity about his legs, about how he got from one place to another, whether he was able to ride a mule, and so on. But of course the boy was nervous. He was seeing his uncle for the first time in all his life, an uncle who was distinctly queer— perhaps even grotesque—in appearance. And the boy no doubt felt neglected, wondering why this uncle of his blood had not come to see him before. Most importantly, most simply, he was a boy of twelve years, compelled by the animal energy in his blood. He had more urgent necessities than to hear music, or to keep still.

Raymi said little. She ate almost nothing, silently observing this long-delayed encounter between father and son.

After the boy finished his dinner he stood. "Mamá, I would like to go now."

"Where will you be going, Yari?"

"To my friends. I told them I would be meeting them."

"Muy bien. Do not come back late, my son."

"I won't. Goodbye, Uncle."

"Goodbye, Yari."

The boy left.

Neither Manco nor Raymi spoke for a time.

"He is a fine-looking boy. As you said."

"Yes. My greatest wish is for you and Yari to care for each other. And for Yari to respect you."

Manco looked at her. "Why is that of such importance to you?"

The question seemed to unsettle her. "I—I want him to learn from you, Manco. There is so much Yari can learn from you."

"Right now it is, I think, most necessary for him to learn from his blood."

Raymi recoiled.

"I do not mean the fact that we are brother and sister, Raymi. I mean the natural blood of the young animal. Yari must ride that animal until he becomes weary of riding. Or until that animal topples him."

"I see. Perhaps this is so."

"With me it was not so because of the legs. I was forced to still the mind while my body was yet filled with its animal blood. I think one must recognize this flooding and ebbing of the blood, even as the fisher observes the tides. For your—our son, there is yet time."

"Time?"

"Yes. In time Yari may come to understand the necessity for stillness."

"As you have learned, Manco."

"I have not entirely learned it, Raymi. But I am fortunate to have a friend and teacher who has helped me. By his own example."

"His name is?"

"Inti. He is a harpist."

"And how did you come to know this man, Manco?"

Manco related to his sister his first encounter with the harpist on the Altiplano. He described his sensation of the music locked in his chest, as if it were a bird beating its wings in a cage. He told of going to the village of Oroya and finding his quena in the wooden ruin of the rubbish yard. He spoke too of the campesino, who, while they were passing Lake Titicaca on the way to Puno, related the fable of the great bird who carried the sun aloft, only to return with it to its resting place in the Lago. And even as the sun fell and rose naturally, rhythmically, so too was there a music that not only sang of life's sorrow—yaravi; but of the joy of the newborn sun. This music was called wayno. Manco paused. Finally he told of going with Tana to Cuzco, and meeting Inti. He did not speak of his time in Tacna.

Raymi listened intently, looking at him steadily as he spoke. Manco saw in her eyes the same light he had seen in Aunt Soledad's eyes when she took hold of his, and Pepito's, hand.

"And now?" she asked.

"Now I play music."

"This bird locked within your chest, my brother: has it been set free?"

Manco looked at her for a moment without answering. It was as if the sheen in her eyes were flowing into his own. Or as if he were gazing into his own eyes.

"No," he said softly. "It has not been finally set free."

That night Manco slept in Tana's hut. The following morning he left with another group of carretas for Cuzco. He thought of Raymi. After a difficulty at the start, their meeting had been peaceful. They were not only brother and sister but, Manco felt, brother and sister of the spirit. And he thought of course of his son. That Yari was healthy and physically strong was a great relief to him. There was, though, something disturbing in the boy's nature, or at least something in his nature that unsettled Manco. But this might have been because of the unusual circumstances of their meeting. Manco had left with the promise of visiting again.

Manco arrived in the city of Cuzco late at night. As the mule on which he had gotten a ride was approaching the hut, he heard Inti's harp. He was playing yaravi. Manco entered softly and sat on the floor. After a few moments Inti gestured for Manco to join him. The two of them played for some time . . . Inti raised his head.

"Cojito, how was the visit?"

"It was better, more peaceful, than I had expected, my friend."

"I am glad."

Manco heard something in his friend's voice. "What is it, Inti?"

"The llama is dead. He died while you were gone. We have already put him under the ground."

Manco did not speak. He was saddened.

"I found him at dawn behind the hut. He lay on his side," Inti said. "The life was gone from him."

IX TOTEM

When Manco awoke the following dawn, Inti was already up.

"You are going to the Quechua Plaza, Inti?"

"Yes. Of course. Are you not going?"

"I do not know. I think it is too great a distance for me, my friend. Perhaps we should consider acquiring an animal. Another llama."

"Let us consider this, Cojito. But for the present I will serve as that animal."

Manco looked at him. "Do you mean what you say, Inti?"

Inti smiled. "Yes. Why not? I have a strong back, and your keen eyes will see for both of us. And we will have the advantage of being able to converse together. Let us try it, my friend."

Inti kneeled and Manco hoisted himself onto the old man's back. Inti straightened easily. He walked a little.

"It is good," Inti said. "You will have to carry the harp. Lean it against my back . . . Yes. Is it good for you?"

"Yes. But what will the people say? They will not know what to make of us."

"You are right, Cojito. They will not know what to

make of us. At first. So they will smile, they will ask questions, and they will at last grow accustomed to us. But now I will set you down so that you can put on your poncho. It is a fine day, is it not?"

"Yes," Manco said, glancing outside through the wooden window. "It is clear and mild."

Manco poured water from a large pot into a smaller pot and washed his face and hands. Then he put on his poncho and chullo.

"It is," Inti said, "a fine day for making music."

Events transpired as Inti had foreseen: the smiles, the questions, the growing accustomed. Manco himself grew accustomed not only to his extraordinary "mount," but to the fact of his old friend's strength. Each morning it was the trek uphill to the Quechua Plaza; back again in the afternoon; and then, when the sun was declining, down to the Plaza de Armas; to return again at night.

In the Plaza de Armas there were always people who had never seen them, who smiled and pointed and asked questions. It was of course natural to express surprise at the single figure of the two men, each dressed in brown poncho and chullo, the uppermost one legless, balancing the harp against the other's back—this single figure moving deliberately down the hillside, framed by the sierra, by the waning sun.

But for the death of the llama, their life continued generally in the old way. They played their music. People visited them in their hut, sitting with them on the earthen floor. One difference was that now many more visitors than previously asked their advice about matters which had little or nothing to do with their music. The fact was that certain people began to look on the two Indios as "sagrado," the very word Raymi had used. Manco assumed that this had come about largely as a result of their physical appearance while walking. He himself had more than once been taken aback at the single shadow they cast. It was perhaps understandable then that others would see in their aspect something magical. Manco was however uncomfortable in the role of wise man or brujo, and he did not know how to answer their questions. He confessed his unease to Inti.

"There is nothing to answer, my friend."

"I do not understand."

"What our questioners want is a portion of that space we share in our music, and that we share now outside the music. They recognize this. They would like to witness it."

"How then can they 'witness' this space, Inti?"

"By being in its presence, my friend. The more power-fully you are joined to it, the more clearly they will recognize it. And some will witness. Those who have moved from listening to hearing will witness."

Manco had at last come to merge with his music. When they played yaravi in the Plaza de Armas Manco occupied that pure space of the waning sun, untouched by the noise in the plaza. And when they played wayno Manco was in the place of newborn light, like a bird in a treetop at dawn. It was not as if he, who for so many years had been pressing, pressing to merge with this space—had finally broken through. Not at all. It was simply that one afternoon Manco put his quena to his lips, and was there. A still brook touched by the dying light. And when, that same afternoon, he played wayno, he was a stream, rain-fed, coursing down-mountain in the early sun.

And when he was not playing, that pure space was yet there as a place of steadiness, of light. Manco had only to imagine his music to be transported there. Thus when his mind turned to his son or to his sister, it turned to them with naturalness, as a bird might fly from a ridge of the sierra to a branch of a tree. That pressure or tightness in his chest, which he had experienced intermittently since he was a child on the Altiplano, had vanished. No longer was it necessary for him to work at amiability with people who could not hear or even listen to his music. He merely was with them as he was without them, or with others who did hear. He merely was.

And now he knew. He knew where Inti was when bent over his harp he played the music. He knew now what

Inti had meant when many years ago he spoke through his music to the crippled boy on the Altiplano, saying, "Yaravi is of the mountain which is born of the earth and brushes the sky."

How Manco had come to this "place," why his own particular trail had been so full of turns and hindrances, and what the specific meaning of each turn and hindrance was—this he did not know. Nor was it of any real importance. One event, long forgotten, Manco did now recall with special vividness: as a child in the hills above the city he had heard somewhere the music of the yaravi played on a quena. The wonderful sadness of this music had taken hold of him, and the next morning he managed to obtain, through the aid of an old herb-woman, a quena made of cone wood. The child did not obtain this quena with soles, but with the promise of doing "tasks." When the old woman asked whether he had the money to buy the instrument, he said no, but that he could do "tasks," and on the strength of this promise the old woman motioned him into a dark opening, a corridor, where he eventually came upon an old blind man who played the yaravi for him, and then gave him the quena, wet with his saliva. Then came the great shaking of the earth. Everything of significance that followed was, Manco saw, somehow prefigured in the child's promise. The music, the pena, Inti . . .

Inti was now an old man. The lines of age were traced on his face. His fingers were not so flexible as they had been, and when they caressed the harp it was with greater economy, with as much attention given to the resonating intervals between notes as to the notes themselves. The effect was no less impressive. Manco knew that his cherished friend was himself preparing to enter this space that echoed silently.

And yet Inti continued to carry Manco on his shoulders, slowly but, as far as Manco could determine, tirelessly. The fact was that Manco too had been brushed by age. His hands and arms were not nearly so strong as formerly, and, with his stumps useless, he could no longer easily maintain his balance on the back of an animal. Nei-

ther the waning strength in his arms, nor the uselessness of
his stumps was of any importance when Manco was with
the music. When he played, the quena became his arm, or
wing, transporting him to that place of the cóndor in the
sierra, which was also hut and tree and lago and the space
in his chest.

His old earnest intention of being *heard* by the borrachos, his compadres drunk on chicha, their bodies jerking in the gutter—this intention was not realized. Manco's
music was powerless to relieve their pain. He accepted this
hard fact resignedly.

Three more times he returned to Puno to visit his sister
and son. And on these occasions he saw clearly that Raymi
was not well, that she would not live much longer. She
herself knew this and it accounted for her continuing,
though unstated, anxiety about her son's relationship with
Manco.

Yari, during these recent visits, seemed just as he was
when Manco had seen him for the first time two years
before: restless, inattentive, demanding, and somewhat
peevish in his manner. Though Manco did not convey his
thoughts to his sister, he was concerned about his son. He
knew that Raymi would soon depart, that Yari would then
be in his charge, and that given the situation, he might not
prove a capable father to his son. Old, crippled, residing in
a hut barren of all but the barest necessities, what could he
offer to such a boy?

Manco spoke of his concern to Inti.

"You are his father," Inti said. "And you will do what
you can when the time comes. But the time has not yet
come, my friend. It is as though a man is following a narrow
trail in the sierra. On one side is the sheer drop to the
canyon thousands of meters beneath. On his other side is a
raging river, fed by the rain. The man neither worries about
falling into the canyon, nor into the river. He has already
established that they are on either side of him, so he con-
centrates only on the trail. If it comes to pass that he must at
some point ford the river, he will do so. If it happens that he
will come to a gap in the mountain with only the canyon

beneath him, he will leap to the other side of the mountain, or he will construct a bridge. Or it may be that he will need to retrace his steps and find an alternate trail. "That trail is your music, Cojito. When you play your quena, remain with the music. If your quena is lost or stolen, or the Quechua Plaza is transformed into a hotel for the turistas—that is something that will concern you when it occurs. It is not wise to push at time, my friend."

As he had done so many times, Manco gratefully accepted his friend's counsel. At first he needed to make a special effort to keep from "pushing at time," from occupying his mind with his sister's eventual death, and with his son. But after a while he succeeded in following his "trail" without strain or anxiety.

Other aspects of Inti's teachings Manco learned and absorbed with less effort. In the gathering of herbs, for example, the trek up to the farthermost hills of the city was too far for Inti to carry his friend. Manco, then, went alone, every twelfth day, procuring a ride on a cart, or when his arms felt strong, on the back of a mule or llama. He knew which herbs were ready and the proper manner in which to gather them. He knew how to strip the resinous bark from a certain cone tree without injuring the tree. He knew where to find the rare shrub wood that Inti called palo de vida. And once back at the hut, Manco knew how to cure the herbs, and how to combine and apply them.

From Inti Manco also learned to be still. Not merely to speak only when necessary, but to speak softly and precisely, out of stillness. This stillness Manco imagined as a lago, calm, yet pulsing with energy beneath. Each spoken word, each utterance, was as a ripple, surrounded by stillness, re-absorbed into it. The lago was of course never entirely still, as the body was not, yet the constant pulse of the water, like the blood flowing through the veins—were sounds of stillness. These sounds defined the space they surrounded, and the surrounding space.

The visits from people who listened to their music, and from people who never listened to their music, but heard about it from others—these visits to the Indios' hut continued. Most of those who came did not return, dissatisfied that the two old "brujos" could not give them the word they thought they were seeking. The single word that would insure their well-being.

Others, sitting quietly, listened to their music, and remained quiet when the music ceased. These others came time and again until most of them too ceased to come.

Of those who continued to come, a few among them suspected that as pleasing as it was to listen, there was something beyond the listening. And of these few, perhaps one or two learned to hear, to witness.

What did it mean to witness?

It meant, for Manco, the recognition of the bond that existed among all things of this earth, living or dead. This witnessing, however it was defined, might be so powerful as to remain with the person indefinitely. Or it might fade. It might be channeled into the hearer's own music or art. Or reside in his living from day to day, from minute to minute.

Among the visitors were two Quechuas with cropped hair and brass buttons, both representatives of the Ejército de Salvación. Manco of course recognized the costumes, the gestures, the words, from his previous encounters with such people. They were planning to hold a "service" in the Indio Iglesia in the hills, and they asked whether the two músicos would perform at their service.

"Why do you ask us?" Inti inquired.

"We ask you because the people love your music."

"We are not Christians," Inti said.

"Are you certain of that, my friend? Many of us are members of Christ's soldiery without fully realizing it. It may be that once you hear our service you may come to such a realization. Though you are an old man, there is yet time."

Inti smiled. He asked on what day the service would be held.

"Tomorrow, at three o'clock, compadre. You will then perform for Christ? For the pobres, our brothers and sisters who are as yet untouched by the grace of El Señor?"

"We will consider it. Tomorrow morning you will find

us in the Quechua Plaza. We will inform you then of our decision."

This did not entirely satisfy the cropped heads. "Are you certain that you cannot tell us now so that we might make arrangements?"

"I wish to discuss this with my friend," Inti said. "Tomorrow morning will be as soon as we can tell you."

"Está bien."

After they left Manco expressed his surprise at Inti's response. "What have these Ejércitos to do with the pobres they claim they wish to save?"

"The Iglesia where this service is to be held is the one where the Sinchi procession ended on the day you returned to Cuzco. Do you recall, my friend?"

"Yes."

"It is also the Iglesia whose door you examined so closely. The door that contains two crucifixions, one for the eyes of those who can see. The other for those who cannot."

"The crucified Cristo is an Indio and his tormentors are conquistadores."

"That is so, Cojito. But it is not so to these people of the Ejército. And if we were to perform for this service we would be doing two services. One for the Ejércitos and the other for the Quechuas, or for those of them who will hear us."

"Ah. But will the Quechuas not assume that because our music is a part of their service, it is the Ejército itself to which they are listening?"

"Those who feel so are perhaps the same who would join the Ejército without the music, or with other music. Those who listen with unspoiled ears will see their mountain."

The following afternoon, seated not on the chairs the Ejércitos had provided, but on the floor between the two aisles, their backs to the altar, the musicians played as their people slowly filed into the Iglesia. The Ejércitos had wanted them to play certain "himnos" in addition to the music they usually played, but Inti said they would perform only if he and Manco were wholly responsible for their music.

As the mothers with their infants wrapped in rebozos on their backs, and their husbands, and the viejos timidly took their seats on the hard wooden pew-chairs, the musicians played yaravi. The effect of the slow plaintive measures echoing in the high enclosed space was stirring even to Manco's ears. Then he remembered: it was in such a place many years ago, when he was a child in the city of Cuzco, that he had heard the yaravi. He had accompanied his parents to the Ejército's service, and was unhappy being there—until he heard the music, the proud plaintive music of the quena playing yaravi. That must have been the beginning, because it was the very next morning that he procured his quena with the promise of doing "tasks."

As he played Manco gazed at the faces of the Quechuas, wondering how many of them heard. And of the young ones who heard, which of them would begin, as he had begun, the fateful journey forward in order at last to return to the beginning.

When the músicos set out on a typical morning, Manco mounted on his friend's back and holding the harp, children from the Indio quarter would follow them, or circle them, singing and dancing. And, as in Puno years before, some of the Quechua women would touch Manco's stumps for good luck.

Once in the small plaza, they moved to their accustomed place near the broken waterless fountain and played. Sometimes other Quechua musicians would join them. And the Indios making their way through the plaza with wood or potatoes or onions on their backs would often set down their bundles and listen to the music. The very young children, who were unaccustomed to listening with their ears, darted back and forth, or played at kick-ball with a rolled up newspaper, laughing, their laughter merging with the lilting notes of the wayno.

In the afternoon, after a little food and rest in their hut, they commenced the trek downhill to the Plaza de Armas, which Inti still referred to by the Quechua name of

Wakaypata. There, among the Cruces and Gringos, they were not touched, but questioned. And they were photographed. Manco did not like being photographed, but Inti hardly seemed to notice. And when they were photographed while playing, Manco himself scarcely noticed. In this plaza too the Indios paused on their uphill climb, set down their loads, and listened, their faces unexpressive but for their eyes. The Gringos milled about with their maps and packages, they snapped photos, they moved back and forth through the plaza. They were restless, intent on seeing everything they had planned to see during their four or five days in the city of Cuzco.

The other Gringos with the long hair and ponchos and beads, who were nearly always young, listened more easily, and a few of them heard—though many more pretended to hear. And some, with their own instruments, would play with the musicians. Usually these young Gringos remained five or ten days in Cuzco, went to Machupicchu, and then to Bolivia. Perhaps their interest in the music continued; Manco did not believe so.

These observations Manco made over a period of years. He was no longer especially interested in reflecting on these matters. But for an exceptional circumstance, he played his music with his back straight and his eyes closed, with concentration and stillness.

Late in the evening they returned uphill to their hut. Often there were visitors waiting for them, but the musicians went about their affairs as though they were alone. They talked a little, perhaps they played a little, they were silent.

X THE FATHER

One evening as they were climbing the final hill beneath their hut, Manco had a premonition that something unexpected would happen. In fact two people were waiting for them beside the hut. They were Raymi and the boy. Raymi, wrapped in a rebozo, was lying on the ground. Inti carried her inside and laid her on a mat. Her eyes were closed, but when Manco came close to her she took his hand.

"I wanted to see," she whispered.

Manco looked at her pityingly. She was suffering. She was very close to death.

Yari, aware that his mother was dying, stood off in a corner of the room, his eyes glazed.

"How did you get here, Yari?"

"In a carreta. I told her no, Uncle, but she insisted on coming."

"Manco," Raymi whispered.

"Yes, Raymi."

"When I am gone place me in the hills. With our people."

Manco nodded.

"Manco."

"Yes, my sister."

"Play yaravi for me. And for Yari. It has been so long."

"I will."

Manco took up his quena and played softly. He glanced at his son who still seemed dazed, as if in shock. He looked into Raymi's eyes which were lit with a faint moist sheen. The life was slowly leaving her face. Manco played, his eyes partially open, looking at her.

"Yaravi," she whispered urgently, trying to raise her head. She meant her son, who was sitting clutching his knees in a corner, unable to come to her. Raymi turned again to Manco and was gazing at him beseechingly as the light drained from her eyes and her pain at last departed.

Manco continued to play softly as the shudders passed through her body. She was gone. Manco set down his quena and gently closed her eyes.

The following day at sunset Raymi was buried in the hills of the city, near the cone forest where Manco and his father and perhaps Raymi too had in an earlier life gone to gather wood. Manco and Inti played yaravi as she was lowered in a simple cone wood casket into the earth. They played as the loose earth was shoveled on top of her.

Yaravi the son attended the funeral, but with the same dazed expression on his face. When Manco spoke some consoling words to him, the boy did not acknowledge them. His pain, Manco knew, was great. He was fourteen years old and evidently had never before seen a human die. Then suddenly to find himself in a situation where he had to travel for three days with his dying mother, only to watch her die—the boy was not yet strong enough to accept this grave reality.

Manco prepared a mat for Yari beneath the window, and he left him food to eat. For three days the boy slept and ate and didn't speak. When Inti and Manco left for the Quechua Plaza the boy was still asleep. When they returned in the afternoon he was awake, lying silently on the mat. And when they returned in the evening he was again asleep.

On the fourth evening the musicians returned at evening to find the boy gone. He did not return that night. He did not return until the following afternoon.

Manco did not ask his son why he had been gone so long, or where he had been. He offered the boy some maté.

"Come, Yari, have some tea with Inti and me."

The boy merely looked at him sulkily.

"Or would you like to eat something? Perhaps you are hungry."

"Yes, I am hungry," Yari said.

"Then I will prepare some chupe," Manco said. He slid along the floor to the hearth, put some potatoes and cheese and herbs in a pot filled with water, stirred the fire, and set the pot on the hearth. As he moved Manco felt his son's eyes on him. He knew that his son was repelled by his halting, crippled movements, and for the first time in many years Manco felt a painful self-consciousness.

Inti, meanwhile, had sat on the floor, and begun to play on his harp.

When the soup was prepared, Manco and Inti ate on the floor while the son sat on the single small chair and ate hungrily, rapidly.

"Have some more chupe if you are still hungry, Yari."

The boy neither responded nor moved from his chair.

That evening three Gringos who had listened to the musicians in the Plaza de Armas, visited the hut. They asked the musicians a few questions about Cuzco, and about the music of the Quechuas. Then Manco and Inti played. As he played Manco opened his eyes a little and for an instant confused the youngest Gringo sitting attentively on the floor, with his son who was still sitting on the chair with the empty soup bowl on his lap, his ears stubbornly closed to the music. Manco closed his eyes.

The next morning as Yari lay asleep on the mat, Manco looked at him. The boy lay on his side with one hand curled under his ear, his long delicate eyelashes resting on his fine smooth face. To Manco's eyes, his son looked like Raymi, the young and beautiful Raymi who had tantalized him with her beauty. Manco's love for his son welled up inside his chest; gently, he brushed the boy's hair.

When the musicians returned from the Quechua Plaza in the afternoon, the boy was gone. And when they returned at evening the boy was still gone. Manco noticed an empty but unwashed bowl on the floor by Yari's mat. His son had returned while the musicians were still in the Plaza de Armas, eaten, then left again.

Manco drank his maté in silence, waiting, hoping for the boy to return. He did not return until the following afternoon. He was lying on his mat when the Indios entered the hut. Again Manco neither scolded nor questioned the boy.

"Hola, Yari," he greeted.

"Hola," his son replied listlessly.

Manco did not know what else to say.

"A cup of maté, Yari?"

"I do not want maté," the boy responded, turning his back to Manco.

That evening when the musicians returned from the large plaza, the boy was again gone.

This continued. For several months the boy appeared and disappeared, responded peevishly, sulked, and silently refused to do any of the chores. Still Manco waited in the hope that Yari's grief would at last subside, and that the boy would learn to accept him and the situation in which he now lived.

Once, Manco asked the boy whether he wished to accompany him into the hills and cone forest to gather herbs, and to his surprise the boy responded affirmatively. While Inti played in the small plaza, Manco and Yari waited by the winding dirt road for a carreta.

As they were riding in the direction of the cone forest, Manco thought of his own father and how fine it was going with him to split and gather the cone wood. He remembered his father's quiet but unmistakeable love for his son as he walked ahead with the rope wrapped about his waist. It was such a love that Manco felt for his own son, and perhaps Yari had at last let go of the great pena produced by his mother's death, and would accept Manco's love. The carreta stopped and father and son slipped down.

As Manco slid along the ground, Yari walked restlessly ahead. Once Manco lost him altogether in the garúa-mist, but then found him again sitting on a stone.

"From this manzanilla," Manco pointed to a flowering plant growing in clusters, "we will make a maté. You can smell how fine it is, Yari. We will cure it in the sun and then we will combine it with herba buena and the leaves of the coca plant. If the sun is yet strong when we return we can prepare the maté tonight."

Manco carefully uprooted the manzanilla and placed the stalks in his bolsa. When he glanced up he saw that Yari was walking away from him.

"Do not walk too far, Yari. It is difficult to see in the garúa."

The boy gestured with his hand impatiently, as if to say: "I can take care of myself."

Manco gathered the manzanilla and another herb growing nearby. Then he slid towards the area of the cone forest. He did not see his son. In the forest he deftly peeled the bark from a particular tree, and then cut some twigs of palo de vida. Finally, farther into the forest, he removed some moss from where it grew about a large tree, using the machete carefully so as not to harm the tiny scale-like leaves. As he made his way out of the forest, the mist had lifted. He did not see his son. Several times he called his name, but heard only the distant echoing of his own voice.

Waiting alone by the side of the dirt road for a carreta to take him back to the hut, Manco recalled his old loneliness as he waited beside the Altiplano road that led to Oroya: a small boy balanced on forked sticks, his chest heavy with the pena of his unreleased love. That love was the music of the yaravi, which Manco imagined as a songbird beating its wings, wanting to be freed. The love throbbing in his chest now was once again Yaravi, his son restlessly beating his wings, wanting to be set free from an uncle who oppressed him. It was the circle. Manco smiled wearily. Always the circle. Only instead of being securely, airily within it, Manco had again been thrust outside. And he was as lost and bewildered now as he had been as a boy on the Altiplano. Perhaps more so, because now his great consuming love had an object, his son, who for every testimony of his father's affection, pushed farther and farther out of reach.

When Manco returned to the hut, Inti heard that he was alone and he felt his friend's distress. Inti had silently observed Manco's growing frustration and isolating love from the time Yari first arrived. But he did not speak about this with his friend. Manco's heart was too full of his love for Inti's words to have any effect. But now Manco confided in him. He told him his son had again disappeared.

"As my love grows, his contempt for me increases," Manco said softly, with emotion in his throat.

"I have seen this."

"What then should I do, my friend?"

"What can you do? You must go on as before. Since you cannot undo what is done, let this love you feel for your son alone. Try to stop feeding it, because the more your son recedes from you, the more this love will feed on itself. It will consume you, Cojito."

"Yes. Yes. I know this even as I act otherwise. It is that I feel he also will learn to hear, to understand the music."

"It may be, my friend. It may be that Yari will come to hear. But if he does it will be in his own time. Who knows better than you how long, how arduous, how full of obstacles this journey into the music is? Though it be with him every day, it is possible that he, like you, will have to travel very far and long in order to return to the very hut he left because he was not yet ready to hear. What after all can he learn now from us, two old and crippled beggars who play a few tunes for centavos; who eat potatoes and herbs and sleep on the floor?"

Manco listened attentively to his friend's words. He knew that Inti was right. And yet something in him could not wholly accept this counsel. Something in him resisted.

"I have tried hard not to demand anything of him," Manco said. "I have tried not to demean him in any way. I have offered him my love without restrictions."

"That is so, Cojito. And yet it is not entirely so. It is the very unselfishness of your love that shames the boy. Because he does not allow himself to feel love for you, every selfless gesture of your own love galls and shames him, increases his guilt. So that your gentleness and concern for his feelings only serve to tighten the chain."

His friend's words pained him. And because they were true, they even angered him a little. Never before had he felt anger towards Inti.

Not that evening, but the next, Yari returned. He returned without a word and lay on his mat. Looking at him closely Manco saw what Inti had long ago seen: his son was shamed. The contempt, the peevishness, both of which were already familiar to Manco, were expressed in the boy's face. But the shame of responding ungratefully to his "uncle's" kindness, this was also there.

Manco did not disturb his son's silence that evening, but the next morning, as they were preparing to leave for the plaza, Manco woke the boy, whose face, fresh from sleep, was wild and lovely and terrified. Manco felt his love push up at his throat. He remembered what he wanted to ask of him.

"Yari, I would like you to prepare the hearth with cone wood and palo de vida. And the herbs that are for curing outside, please take them into the hut when the sun is at the highest, or very soon afterwards."

The boy, perhaps not fully awake, glared at him without responding.

These tasks that Manco had assigned were of no real urgency. He himself usually prepared the hearth, and if the herbs remained some few hours longer in the sun, their usefulness would not be much diminished. But Manco had decided to change his approach to his son. For many months he had demanded nothing while being painstakingly attentive to the boy's feelings. After Inti had pointed out his error, Manco decided that henceforth he would exercise certain fatherly privileges, such as enlisting his son in the chores of the hut.

When the musicians returned from the plaza, Manco's fearful, unadmitted expectation had been realized: the boy was gone, the assigned chores remained to be done. Manco brought the dried herbs into the hut and set about preparing the hearth. He and Inti drank their tea in silence. Afterwards Manco sat outside beneath the hut and looked out over the hills. He closed his eyes and dozed a little. When he opened his eyes the light had changed and Manco forgot where he was. For a moment he imagined himself in Puno, sitting beneath the chaki's hut, waiting impatiently for Raymi to return. With a full and aching chest, waiting.

Manco had very nearly concluded that he would never again see his son, when the boy returned four days after he had left. His poncho was rent, he was very dirty, and his nose and eyes were dripping, as if he had been sleeping outside in the cold. Again Manco's love surged up inside him. Quietly he brought the boy food and maté, and when Yari lay down and slept, Manco settled his own poncho about his son.

The following morning, instead of going with Inti to the Quechua Plaza, Manco got a ride to the large market near the Plaza de Armas. There he purchased a poncho woven from the best alpaca wool. When he returned to the hut Yari was still asleep. Manco sat on the floor and observed his son as he slept silently, his face composed and childlike. If only this childlike trust were there in his waking—but soon as he awoke his face would take on the sulky, contemptuous mask. Manco had seen it happen many times.

The boy awoke, he saw his father, his face changed. "How do you feel this morning, Yari?"

Yari looked at him confusedly. "Why are you here? What hour is it?"

"It is late morning. I have brought you something from the large mercado." Manco held up the poncho. He spread it on the boy's mat.

Yari touched the poncho with his fingers, even as he continued to look at his father. Manco watched his son's eyes fill with water—then abruptly clear, become hard.

"Gracias," Yari said, twisting his body away.

"May it bring you good fortune, my son." Manco did not realize what he had said until the words were out of his mouth.

Yari heard the words and turned to Manco; his face was puzzled.

"I am sorry, Yari, but that is how I sometimes think of you, as my son."

They stared into each other's eyes silently. Then Yari turned away again.

Manco left the hut and sat outside on the ground. He was still sitting when he saw Inti above him, carrying his harp and a long stick, making his way slowly towards the hut. Manco did not recall when he had last seen his friend from such a distance. Seeing him now Manco was struck at how old and frail Inti appeared. The sun, high and bright in the cloudless sky, enveloped the old man's head and shoulders so that Manco could not see Inti's face. It was not necessary; in the many years of their friendship Manco had rarely seen his expression waver. When he was at his harp there was in his face a rich emptiness, a calm radiance. When he was not playing it was the same. And yet as Manco observed Inti, now close to him, he knew that his old friend's body was dying.

"Cojito," Inti said, as he came up to the hut.

"Yes, my friend. I am sitting here."

Inti sat down beside him. The two Indios sat silently, Inti with his sightless eyes lowered, Manco staring blankly into the distance. As they were sitting Yari emerged from the hut wearing his old rent poncho. When the boy saw them he turned away, but then turned back, and standing in front of Manco, he said: "I am going away. I am not happy here and so I am going away."

He was about to say more but changed his mind, wheeled away from them and ran down the hill.

Manco watched his son run, then walk, then run again down the winding hills in the direction of the Plaza de Armas.

When the boy disappeared from sight, Manco made his way back into the hut. The poncho he had purchased for his son was still lying on the boy's mat. Manco sat on the mat and moved his hand along the bast surface. He thought he could feel the warmth of his son's body on the mat. He felt the poncho with his fingers.

Inti came into the hut. He placed his harp down and sat on the floor.

"He has gone, Inti."

"Yes."

Manco told his friend that he had addressed the boy as "my son." "The words were out before I could stop them. Perhaps that is what drove him away."

Inti did not speak.

"The boy rent his poncho. He will not keep out the cold with such a garment, Inti." He paused. "I remember," he continued softly, "how grateful I had been when the campesino gave me his chullo. This was many years ago, when I came to the village of Oroya from the Altiplano. I wore the chullo for many winters. And then when I was in Tacna the campesino left me the quena made of bone . . ."

Manco stopped talking, he covered his face with his hands.

Still Inti did not speak.

Manco looked up at him. "Inti, I am going after him."

"Do you think that is wise, Cojito?"

"His mother placed him in my charge, Inti. He is my son."

"Yes."

"He could not have gotten far. He is without money. And he does not know how to beg. He may have gotten no farther than the large plaza. I will wait for a carreta beside the road."

"You will wait a long time at this hour, my friend. I will be going to the Wakaypata as usual and I will carry you there."

"I am most grateful, Inti."

Manco sat anxiously on Inti's shoulders for what seemed an interminable time. When they approached the plaza Manco looked about. And once by the fountain, he scoured the entire area with his eyes. It had become colder, and fewer people than usual were in the vicinity. Yari was not among them.

Manco saw an acquaintance of his, an Indio herb-seller on his mule. Manco called to him.

"Kenkko, will you take me on the mule? I am trying to find my nephew. I think he is somewhere in the area."

"I will gladly, my friend. But will you be able to stay on?"

"I will stay on," Manco said.

Kenkko lifted him onto the mule behind him, and they started out of the plaza. Manco felt the uselessness of his stumps. He had to maintain his balance by clasping Kenkko's waist, which was difficult.

"Let me sit in front of you, Kenkko. That way I can take hold of the reins."

"As you wish, my friend." Kenkko lifted Manco and set him down in front of him.

The force of Kenkko's body behind made it easier for Manco to stay seated on the animal.

"Where then?"

"Go down Calle La Campaña," Manco directed.

This was a long street that wound for a kilometer to the westernmost margin of the city.

The two hours of siesta had not yet ended so that the streets were comparatively empty. Also it had begun to rain. Manco did not see his son. When they got to the end of the street Manco directed Kenkko up an adjacent street. It was raining harder.

"It is not likely your nephew would remain outside in the rain, Cojito."

Manco was scarcely listening. "Please, Kenkko, go down Calle La Merced at the southern side of the plaza."

"As you wish, Cojito."

This too was a long street, with a high ancient wall on one side. Manco did not see his son.

When they got to where the street widened into the campo on the outskirts of the city, Manco told the Indio to set him down.

"Here, my friend? What will you do here?"

Manco did not respond. He was thinking of Raymi, of her eyes as she listened to him play yaravi beneath the chaki's hut. He was thinking of the inflamed eyes of his son . . .

Kenkko set him down on the campo.

"Está bien? Will you be all right here, Cojito?"

"I will. Thank you, Kenkko."

"I am always happy to serve you, my friend."

Manco sat on the ground in the rain. He imagined his son with his unhappy inflamed eyes, cold and miserable and alone, walking aimlessly in the city. He loved the boy. He loved Yari as he had loved the boy's mother. And when he thought of his son the face and eyes belonged as well to Raymi. That surging sorrowful love that had possessed him long after the intimacy with Raymi, that he had managed finally to contain—this was what he felt now for his son. Yet even as Manco was blinded by his passion he recognized its futility. Of course Yari had to go his own way, suffer the penas of his unbridled nature as countless others had done and would continue to do. Had not Manco recognized this almost at once when he saw the boy for the first time several years ago? Manco had told Raymi as much, softening somewhat the burden of his perception so as not to wound her. He had told her that Yari would have to be led by the insistent animal in his blood until he wearied of it—or until it toppled him. Was it not then futile and even selfish for Manco to thrust himself in the boy's heedless path? Manco knew that it was, and yet he could not break the binds of his suffocating love.

It rained harder. The fire cracked in the sky, the thunder responded, and the rain came harder. Manco looked up at the sky but could see nothing through the sudden dark. He felt the water soak through his poncho, and yet he scarcely felt it. He remembered looking into Raymi's eyes when he saw her again after many years—gazing into her eyes and seeing his own. He thought of his father and the cone forest, of the garúa-mist, and Tacna—the cold hard ground of Tacna. And yet the light, the light of the sky in the fountain, the great bird's wing and the humpback. He saw in his mind the laughing face of the Arco del Sol in Oroya. He knew that someplace within him all these images were a single image, unbroken. Again Manco heard the thunder in the skies, feeling on every side of him the shaking of the earth . . .

Manco was either asleep or senseless when he was picked up and carried out of the rain. Two people carried him and he knew without opening his eyes that one of them was Inti. It was too great an effort for him to make out who the other was.

When Manco finally awakened he knew first of all that he was warm. A woolen poncho had been draped over him to keep him warm. Then he saw Inti and he knew that he was lying on his own mat in their hut.

The Indio squatting next to Inti smiled.

"Manco," he said.

Manco looked up at him, trying to focus his eyes. "Pepito?"

"Yes. I have come to the city of Cuzco to play my music," he said seriously.

Manco smiled. He held out his hand and his cousin took hold of it.

"After not finding you in the hut, I was told to go to the Plaza de Armas. There I saw Inti, and since it was raining quite hard we thought that you might have gotten stuck someplace."

"Inti, you followed me," Manco said.

"Yes. When it had begun to rain very hard Pepito and I both followed you."

"You might have drowned there on the campo," Pepito said.

Manco was absentmindedly kneading his poncho covering—when he recognized it as the poncho he had bought for Yari. He recalled now what had happened after he left Inti in the plaza.

"Why are you not on the Altiplano, Pepito?"

"Father died, and since then the brothers have married. There being no need for me anymore, I have come here. I have waited a long time to come to the city of Cuzco, Manco."

"And you have been playing your quena?"

"Yes." He removed the instrument from his poncho and handed it to Manco. "It is the same that you bought for me in Oroya."

Manco saw immediately that Pepito had taken good care of it. He blew into it: the tone was good, clear.

"I have invited Pepito to live with us," Inti said.

"That is good. That is very good," Manco smiled.

Neither Manco nor Inti alluded to Yari. Pepito now slept on Yari's mat and accompanied the musicians at dawn and in the afternoon to the plazas. Pepito played yaravi with tenderness and skill, but that was the single composition he knew. Manco taught him wayno, which he liked at once, and after some months learned to play with a high degree of competence.

Manco found it extraordinary that though he had seen his cousin but twice in the many years since he had left the Altiplano, Pepito seemed precisely as he had been: gentle, trusting, affectionate. He resembled Inti more than he did Manco. Like Inti, Pepito was steady, invariable in his affections, at peace. What he lacked was Inti's dimension. Inti's music resonated quietly beyond itself, creating everywhere echoes of its own likeness. As the sun evoked light from stone, color from the brown hard earth; as the moon cast its beam on the untrodden snow of the highest sierras. Pepito's music did not yet have this dimension, this resonance.

Manco of course was different. He was turbulence, uncertainty, pena. His necessity, as Inti once put it, was to remain on the narrow trail between these obstacles until the trail widened. The trail always widened so long as you continued to follow it. Finally it widened, became water or sky or mountain, while remaining what it always had been: earth, rock, sand. This was so. Manco felt deeply that it was so.

And yet he was still not home. The love he did not speak of with his friend, the consuming love for his son, he still felt. It inspired envy in him when he saw an Indio brush his son's head affectionately; or when he saw a child in his father's arms listening to his music. All around him Manco saw what he had never before seen clearly: love. Yet he himself was void.

When the season of cold came to Cuzco, Manco gave Pepito the poncho he had originally bought for his son. Pepito's own poncho had become badly frayed from too many Altiplano rains and winters.

Inti, who had never before failed to play in the plazas, now remained in the hut more often than he left it. The winter was raw and Inti was very old. Pepito now carried Manco to and from the plazas. Though not tall, Pepito was wide-shouldered and strong, and he carried Manco with little effort. Manco and Pepito played their quenas in the plazas, and they played well together. And when Inti played with them it was better still. But Manco was already silently preparing for his friend and teacher's final departure. He knew it would not be long before Inti would leave not to return. Yet though he worshipped his friend, this anticipation did not especially pain him. Dying, Inti would simply, silently rejoin the circle, the still water of his music.

Although Manco enjoyed playing the music, he was rarely within it. The easy concentration and silent immersion in the music that Manco had experienced in the years after returning from Tacna was gone. The heaviness in his chest pushing up at his throat when he witnessed unhindered love, kept him outside his music. And rather than diminishing with time, the pain became more insistent. Not only a father's love for his son, but visible love of any kind was sufficient to kindle Manco's passion and envy.

One afternoon as he and Pepito were performing in the Plaza de Armas, the anguish took such hold of Manco that he could no longer play. He told Pepito to continue, that he would get a ride back to the hut.

An Indio took him uphill in a small bicycle-driven cart. Manco had already decided he would again search for his son. He would take food and money and he would hire a cart, or even a carro, and he would search for his son who might still be somewhere in the city of Cuzco.

The Indio set him down a few meters from the hut, and as Manco was sliding along the ground he heard Inti's harp playing yaravi. Instead of going inside the hut, Manco sat on the ground and looked in through the open door at his old friend stroking his harp. Once Inti raised his face just slightly and Manco saw that it was radiant. At that instant Manco felt the grief of his friend's leaving. He lowered his head to his chest and listened . . .

He heard the music issuing from beneath the large rock of the sierra on the Altiplano. And as he hobbled back to the pasture area and then rode to the hut, the music echoed about him. Aunt Soledad's eyes, dying on her pallet, were transparent, already within the great circle. Manco listened to the music and watched Raymi's eyes change from fire to reflected fire, like sun on still water. The great Lago between Oroya and Puno was still as the Cóndor slowly descended . . .

Manco saw the faces in the lights of Puno, the hard money-greed faces of the Cruces, and the tender faces of the infants, and the steady peaceful faces of certain of the old ones. Listening to Inti's harp, he heard the music of all these lives growing, dying, at peace, hating, loving. Loving! Did they not all love? The Castellanos, the Cruces, the Indios, the Gringos, the borrachos wailing in their pain in the gutter? The Quechuas who carved their own crucifixion on the Iglesia door: they loved. Every one of them loved. With a love that grew and thrived and died. With a love that died before it flowered. With a love that died even as it was flowering. All love died, and his own unrealized love for his son was not an obstacle to his affection for others—but a bond. Their love too would die, leaving only its reflection, its memory. As a pebble rippled dropping into the still darkness of the water to become one with all things.

Since he lost his legs in the terremoto, Manco had remained separate from all but a few people. This had changed somewhat in Cuzco, performing with Inti, and yet it had not been a real change. He learned to respond more easily, to listen more openly—but he remained essentially separate. And his broken love for his son pulled him even further away . . .

Manco heard the music. The spaces in Inti's music were empty and filled with love. Fired by love: gone, dead, living. It did not matter, for within the circle of the music time was still. All moved about the still center of the circle, and the stillness was love. Long ago Inti had said to the boy that yaravi was of the mountain, which was born of the earth and brushed the sky. All then was joined, not in a chain, but as a semblance each of each other, as the mountain stream reduced sand or stone to water. And if this was so, that joining must be love. How could he not have felt this before? Pepito felt it naturally. The children who danced in a circle about him as he played for them—they felt it instinctively. Perhaps he too had felt it without recognizing it. Now he recognized it.

Inti raised his head. "Cojito."

"Yes, my friend. I am here. I did not wish to interrupt you."

Inti smiled.

Manco made his way inside and sat on the floor facing his friend.

"You have heard the music."

"I have heard it, Inti," Manco said softly. "I have finally heard it."

"That is good. It has begun for you, Cojito."

Manco was silent.

"And for me," Inti said, smiling faintly, "I go now to a new beginning."

"You are going, Inti?"

"Yes, my friend. The carreta will take me to the Lago above Puno. Afterwards I will go to the sierra of the Altiplano."

"The Altiplano? I will find you on the Altiplano, Inti?"

Inti laughed softly. "You will find me in Cuzco, Cojito. You will not fail to find me."

Manco heard these words. He did not speak.

"Hand me my stick, Cojito."

Manco gave Inti his stick.

"Are you going to the road now?"

"I am going to the road, Cojito. I will say goodbye to you, my dear friend."

They embraced.

Manco watched Inti, carrying only his harp and his stick, make his way slowly up the hill. Sitting beneath the hut, Manco watched his old, old friend move slowly away from him, out of sight.

XI WATER

The seasons continued to turn. Tana, the quena-maker, and Tampu stopped at the hut each time they came to Cuzco, and the four Indios played their music together. In the meantime Pepito had also learned how to make quenas. He went with Manco to the cone forest where they chose the proper wood, and Manco instructed Pepito in the use of the tools.

The two cousins played in the Quechua Plaza in the mornings, and in the Plaza de Armas in the afternoons and evenings. On occasion Pepito carried Manco high into the Indio quarter where they played for the old ones and for the children. And when they returned to their hut at night there were often visitors, some of whom wanted "answers" to the large questions that were troubling them. The two Indios had no answers.

As they lived and played together, Pepito came more and more to resemble Inti in Manco's eyes. His music became surer, and the center of his music stiller. And when he was outside the music, the music often remained with him. Unlike Inti, who was eloquent when he chose to speak, Pepito was not at ease with words. So that when there was talking to be done, it was usually Manco who spoke.

Once, as they were playing in the Quechua Plaza in the early morning, an old Indio on a horse and leading a llama, stopped by them to listen to the music. When Manco opened his eyes he saw the old man, but then he closed his eyes again. He and Pepito were playing wayno, moving fluidly from one sparkling embellishment to another, to the delight of those listening and especially the children. When the wayno was over, Manco opened his eyes and looked at the old Indio, who was returning his gaze steadily, without particular expression. He sat straight-backed on his horse and wore his chullo pulled low over his ears. Manco remembered.

"You are the campesino who many years ago took me from the Altiplano to Oroya, and then, later, to the city of Puno. It was you who so generously gave me this quena." He held up the instrument.

"Yes. And how are you, my friend?"

"I am better and better," Manco said.

The campesino laughed. Manco remembered that laugh.

"And yourself?" Manco asked. "How is it with you? Do you still transport cone wood?"

"Yes, of course, my friend. I do as I have always done."

"I am glad to hear it," Manco said. Then he added: "Inti, my old friend, with whom you left the quena for me, has gone."

"I have recently seen him."

Manco was startled. "You have seen Inti?"

"I have. Passing down from Puno. He is by the great water."

"By Lago Titicaca?"

"Claro."

"He is playing there," Manco said.

"That is so, my friend. He is playing his music. As you are. Your quena makes a clear sound."

"Yes. And I thank you for giving it to me." Manco

looked at the llama. "I suppose your llama, the one I remember so well from those times many years ago, is long gone."

"Not at all," the campesino laughed. "He is with me yet. I will have you ride him some day."

"I?"

"Tú mismo—yourself, my friend. I will take you to the water. Or perhaps to the Altiplano. To me it is the same since both are on the way.

Manco heard these words. He turned to Pepito.

"Do you remember this man, my cousin? Many years ago, when you went with me to the road leading out of the Altiplano, it was he who took me."

"I remember," Pepito said softly. "Con mucho gusto, Señor—I am happy to see you again."

"Igualmente—I too," the campesino said. "I heard your wayno and it was very fine. I should like to hear yaravi."

"Of course. With pleasure," Manco said.

He and Pepito played yaravi for the campesino, and for the Indios listening near the fountain and walking through the plaza with wood or produce on their backs, and for whoever else happened to be there and stopped to listen . . .

Other TMP books:

SHE HAD SOME HORSES Joy Harjo
AMERICA MADE ME Hans Koning
ECHOES INSIDE THE LABYRINTH
  Thomas McGrath
FROM SAND CREEK Simon J. Ortiz
THE MOJO HANDS CALL/I MUST GO
  Sterling Plumpp
SOMEHOW WE SURVIVE Sterling
  Plumpp (ed.)

For descriptions of these and other fine
books write to Thunder's Mouth Press,
Box 780, New York City, 10025.

About the Author

Harold Jaffe writes fiction, poetry
and criticism. Besides DOS INDIOS,
he has written MOURNING
CRAZY HORSE (stories), and
MOLE'S PITY (a novel). He has
also edited a nineteenth century
biography of Walt Whitman, and
co-edited three literary anthologies.
He has lived and traveled in Asia
and Central and South America,
and is the recipient of a 1983
National Endowment for the Arts
fellowship for fiction.